I0451829

Couples Swap

Paradise Cruises Series: Book 1

AE Moran

The Invisible Publishing Company

Contents

Chapter 1: Selena

I pause at the edge of the pier and gaze out at the sun sparkling on a crystal blue ocean. "Wow! Look at that!" I breathe. "It's so beautiful!"

"Come on, Selena!" my husband Landon calls down to me. He's already halfway up the gangway to board the cruise ship. "Hurry up or we'll be late!"

I hustle away from the pier railing and have to stop a second time when one of the baggage porters passes me. He wheels an enormous luggage trolley piled to the very top bars with suitcases, bags, and leather cases.

"Oh! Sorry!" I exclaim.

He only nods and keeps on going. He pushes the trolley down a different ramp into the bottom hold of the massive cruise ship parked at the pier.

I pull my carry-on bag up to my shoulder, but I have to stop a third time when I get to the gangway. Another group of people is trying to get up it.

They can't get onto the gangway because Landon is coming down it—going the wrong way. He shoves a few people before he steps onto the pier. Then the other passengers can board.

They shoot both of us dirty looks. "What is taking you so long?!" he hisses. "You know we can't board separately. We have to check in at the same time."

"You could have gone ahead. I could have met you at the top. You didn't have to shove those people."

"Don't start that again," he snaps back. "Now quit stalling and staring into space. We're already late."

I don't answer to tell him what I really think. We aren't late. I have a watch. We have plenty of time. We wind up right behind the other couples in line to check in with the ship's activities coordinator.

She smiles at the people in front of us, gets their names, and checks them off on her clipboard. They pass her to board the ship.

Now it's our turn. We stop at an ornate sign that reads, *Paradise Cruises.*

The coordinator's nametag reads, *Allie Rosche.* "Welcome aboard the *Electric Emerald,*" she tells us. "Can I get your names?"

"Landon and Selena Neise," Landon replies. "We should have an executive suite."

"Yes, Sir, Mr. Neise." She checks off our names. "You're in suite 45A. That's on the top deck, but you'll need to be back down here on the main activity deck in half an hour for your safety briefing and tour." She beams at us. "Have a great voyage."

Landon steps past her and onto the ship's sweeping piazza. It opens into a huge deck with a bunch of pools, fountains, and slides that drop into the kids' pool.

I head for the big windows looking out over the ocean view. There isn't a cloud in the sky. It's a perfect day with a flat sheen of gorgeous blue going all the way to the farthest horizon.

"Look, Landon!" I exclaim. "This is so magnificent! Look at those pools—and there's the golf links on that lower deck! Look, people are playing out there already! I wonder if we can rent clubs if we don't have our own."

"Will you stop it?!" he hisses under his breath again. "You heard what Allie said. We have to check into our suite and come back here for the safety tour. We don't have to look at all that right now."

"We don't have to go up to the suite right now," I counter. "Or you can go up there yourself if you want to put your bag away. I'll stay here and admire the view. Then I won't have to go anywhere for the tour."

He makes a face at me. "Are you going to make this a problem for both of us for the whole trip? I don't know why I decided to come on this trip with you."

I lose my temper, but fortunately, I manage to keep my voice down enough so the other boarding passengers don't hear me.

"This trip was your idea, not mine," I snap. "Don't you dare forget why we're here. We're here because I caught you cheating for the fourth time and you begged me to come on this trip so we could work it out and rebuild our marriage. I was going to leave you because, as far as I'm concerned, it's already over between us. That's why I'm here. So don't give me that crap about me being the problem. You are. I still have time to walk down that gangway and move out of our house if you really want to make this a problem."

He changes his tune instantly. Of course.

"You don't have to do that. I just don't want us to miss the tour." He puts his free hand behind my back. "Come on. Let's go up to the suite and settle in. We can admire the view later."

I throw my elbow at him to shake him off. "Don't you dare touch me, you filthy piece of shit. You're the one who has to work to rebuild our marriage, not me. I'm staying here to admire the view with you or without you. Go to the suite yourself. I have better things to do."

I storm off and leave him standing there. What a creep. The guy can't keep his pants zipped to save his life and he wants to blame me for this? I don't think so.

I don't even care that I'm carrying my bag around. I really would like to put it down somewhere so I don't have to lug it on my shoulder.

I don't turn around to see what Landon is doing while I walk out to the activity deck. I don't want to see him.

I'm just turning off toward the pools when one of the bellboys comes up to me. His nametag reads, *Paul.*

"Could I take your bag for you, Ma'am?" He smiles at me. He's just a young kid, but he has a nice smile. "I can take it to your suite if you want me to."

"Oh! Thank you so much! I really appreciate it." I hand over the bag. "It's Suite 45A."

"No problem. Enjoy your trip."

He walks away and leaves me hands-free. This is perfect. Everything about the ship is perfect.

I walk out to the very prow of the activity deck. The salty wind blows through my hair. I love this. It makes all the dirty business going on in my marriage worthwhile.

I find myself smiling at the ocean, the pools, and the other passengers walking around. Some young kids are already splashing in the kids' pool and sliding down the slide to cannonball into the water.

I turn around to admire the rest of the ship. The piazza sweeps through the main deck and connects with the grand concourse. It covers ten whole decks of stores, casinos, restaurants, and theaters for movies, shows, and comedy clubs.

I can't wait to explore the whole ship. I'm just not looking forward to doing any of that with Landon.

I'm the one who doesn't know why I agreed to come on this trip. He won't say or do anything that will change my mind about ending it.

The trust is gone. No matter what he says or does, I'll never believe he won't cheat on me again. If I stay with him, he'll take that as permission to do it again. He's already done it too many times before.

I just need to move on and start rebuilding my life. I need to get away from him, separate all our assets, and rebuild myself. There is no marriage left to rebuild.

The question is how I'm going to break the news to him. I've already told him how I feel. Agreeing to come on this trip is only giving him false hope.

It's also wasting my time when I could be finding someone who will actually be loyal to me.

I decide to go check out the concourse and maybe a few more of the activities. The ship has a climbing wall, multiple gyms, racquetball courts—literally everything.

The ship gives me a new sense of excitement about rebuilding the life I lost. I've put my own happiness and future on hold for Landon. I need to get that back by exploring other things.

I head for the piazza only to notice a bunch of other passengers gathering around Allie. The safety tour must be starting.

Landon bumps into a few more people when he shoulders his way toward me. I cringe. I'm embarrassed that I'm here with him. I never noticed how rude he is to others.

Did I blind myself to his behavior before? Is that how I wound up with such a loser?

He has the nerve to put his arm around me. I want to shake him off again, but there are too many people around.

I try squirming, but he either doesn't get the message or ignores it.

A six-foot-five beefy guy in an immaculate coal-grey suit comes down the piazza and stands next to Allie. His height and huge shoulders dwarf her by a mile.

He wears his sandy brown hair clipped short in a military style. His sharp blue eyes survey everyone with crisp, alert, hawkish intensity.

Allie gives him the same glowing smile she gave us. He smiles back and nods.

She faces the crowd and raises her voice so we can all hear her. "Welcome aboard your Paradise Cruise Line, everybody! This is your safety briefing and tour of the *Electric Emerald*. As you all know, I'm your activity coordinator, Allie." She lays her hand on the big guy's muscular shoulder. "This is our Chief of Security, Troy Nixon. If you have any issues, requirements, or problems on your voyage, you only have to tell one of us or any of the staff or crew. We're all here to serve you and make sure you all have the time of your lives."

She heads down the piazza and points out the big windows to the right. "If you look over the side on your right here, you'll see the lifeboats. In the event of an emergency, all passengers will assemble here in the breezeway outside the piazza to board the lifeboats. Staff and crew will hand out life vests and other flotation devices before you board. Our emergency procedures require the captain and crew to signal for emergency assistance before anyone leaves the ship, so in the unlikely event that we do need to use the lifeboats, it will only be for a short time before Coast Guard support ships come to pick us up."

She heads out the other side of the piazza to another enormous deck in the ship's rear. Troy stays by her side all the way. He never takes his eyes off the passengers except to cast a sharp, searching glance at the surroundings.

I find myself studying him. He sure acts like he knows what he's doing. I'm glad someone like him is in charge of security on board this ship. He acts like he's on a military mission or something.

Allie waves her hand behind us. "If you look up behind you, you'll see the bridge. That's where the captain and crew steer the ship, navigate our course, and communicate with all coastal authorities for permission to enter the territorial waters of our destination countries."

I find myself getting distracted by more views of the ocean behind the ship. Allie keeps talking about all the features, activities, and safety protocols we need to follow if anything goes wrong.

"Here we have an emergency stop alarm. You'll find these located throughout the vessel and one in each of your cabins. Pressing this big red button will bring the ship to an immediate stop and set off an alarm on all decks and on the bridge to alert the captain and crew of an emergency."

I look up at Landon to see if he notices how beautiful this all is. That's when I see him checking out one of the women near us.

She's a sleek, curvaceous, toned, Latina woman with glistening black hair down to her waist.

She wears ultra-short shorts and a bikini top that leaves absolutely nothing to the imagination.

Landon gives her a seductive look and his eyes shoot down to her cleavage bulging from her top. She blushes and smiles at him.

I elbow him hard in the ribs to make him stop staring at her. He actually has the nerve to glare at me like he wasn't doing anything wrong.

He has to pay attention to the tour when Allie leads us into a different hallway that cuts down the side of the concourse. She shows us the ship's security office.

"If you need to report a security incident, you can come here and check in with Troy or any of the other ship's security personnel....."

I barely look at the security office. I'll probably never need it.

I catch Landon checking out a few other women in the tour group. I don't try to distract him.

We're supposed to be working on our relationship and he's pulling the same crap right here in front of me.

Allie leads the tour through a few more stops and returns to the piazza. She wishes us all a safe and enjoyable voyage and informs us that breakfast, lunch, and dinner are available around the clock in the concourse.

The crowd breaks up. I turn away to go back to the concourse. I have some serious exploring to do.

Landon grabs my arm and pulls me back. "Where are you going?" he demands.

"I'm going exploring. I want to check out the ship—and you certainly look like you have some things you want to check out, too. I'll see you around."

"Hey! Why don't you come with me?"

I make a face. "Why—so I can watch you staring at half-naked women? No, thanks."

He pulls me closer. "Listen. I've been thinking....."

"Living dangerously again? Ha!"

He ignores the jab. "I think we should try a couples swap. What do you say? I'm not checking out other women. I'm checking out other couples."

I stare at him in mounting horror. "A couples swap? Seriously? Do you even know what that means?"

"Of course I do. We hook up with another couple. You sleep with the guy and I sleep with the girl. We get to experience other people and we get to share that excitement and experience with each other." He eases in extra close to my face. "It could be the kick our relationship needs to reignite the passion. What do you think?"

I snort in his face. "I think you're on drugs as usual."

"We could do it all the time. We could become a swinger couple with other partners we see on a regular basis. We wouldn't have to be stuck with only each other all the time. Just try it. You'll see how exciting it is and how much it can enliven our relationship."

"How can you even suggest that, Landon?!" I counter. "The fact that those words even came out of your mouth proves our marriage is over."

"What's the matter now? Just try it. If it doesn't work, we haven't lost anything."

I stare at him as the truth sinks in. It's over. Our marriage can't be saved—not for anything.

He's been sleeping around on me all this time. Now he's trying to get me to do the same thing.

He probably wants to point to me doing it with someone else so he can justify all his past cheating. He can say I have nothing to complain about because I did it, too.

I'm so stunned and heartbroken that I don't move or say anything when he leans in and kisses me on the forehead.

"I'll find a really good couple for us to hook up with," he murmurs. "Don't worry. You don't have to do anything if you don't like the guy—but I have a really good feeling about this. This is going to make us stronger than ever."

He kisses me one more time and walks off somewhere. I'm too dazed even to think straight.

This is the last straw. Now he plans to start doing it with other people right in front of me. I can't sink any lower than this.

I stumble out into the breezeway next to the piazza, collapse onto a bench, and stare out at the beautiful ocean. I'm in one of the most magnificent settings I've ever seen, but I can't enjoy it.

Tears sting my eyes. I'm alone. I've been alone for a long, long time—since long before I found out Landon was cheating on me.

I've been alone in this marriage almost since the beginning. I just didn't know it until right this minute.

He never planned to be faithful to me. He must have married me already knowing he would sleep around. I'm the fool for believing his lies.

I cover my face trying to hold back tears, but I can't—not now when the truth finally hits home. It's over. I'm single. Soon I'll get divorced. I'll be one of those divorced women that no one wants.

He did this to me. He was the one who was supposed to love me forever. Instead, he betrayed me and ruined my life.

Now I really feel how broken and devastated my life is. I really have a long way to go to rebuild my self-confidence.

I need to learn something new about how to choose a partner. I don't want to make the same mistake again.

I can't deal with any of that right now. I just have to sit here and feel how deeply this man has completely crushed my life. I have nothing left.

Chapter 2: Reese

I stop at the bottom of the gangway to check the program on my phone. "This thing is incredible! It has four pools, a golf course, a climbing wall, a gym...."

My girlfriend Zaria gasps and rolls her eyes to Heaven. "Please. You aren't going to spend all your time in the gym, are you?"

"I have to keep up my workouts. I don't want to end up like *that* guy."

I nod toward another passenger boarding the *Electric Emerald,* the Paradise Cruise ship docked at the pier.

The guy wears an enormous Hawaiian shirt that does nothing to hide his belly sagging almost down to his thighs.

Zaria laughs. "I think you can take it easy for a few days, at least. We're supposed to be on vacation here."

I look down at my phone, but I have to pay attention when we get onto the gangway. We wait our turns and check in with the bubbly activity coordinator, Allie.

"All our luggage is already on board the ship," I remark. "We have some time before the safety tour."

"Ooo!" Zaria grabs my arm. "Let's go check out the concourse. I want to see everything."

"You won't be able to see everything in half an hour."

"Come on!" She pulls me into the concourse.

The place is already full of passengers. They shop, eat, drink, gamble, and play games in the fun park arcade.

I stop in front of one of the music venues. "Nothing is on until tonight."

"Let's get a drink. I'm thirsty—and we can get lunch here." Zaria turns in at one of the restaurants.

"It's barely eleven o'clock in the morning," I tell her. "It's too early to drink."

"I mean something non-alcoholic, silly." She shoots me a smirk. "Your mind is already in the gutter. Come on."

We enter the restaurant. A few people stand and sit at the bar and tables. Some of these people are already eating. They must have the same idea about getting lunch before the safety briefing.

I grab a table in the middle of the room and sit down. Zaria goes to the bar to get our drinks.

I look around at all the people. Some are older couples. Some are by themselves or two women together. Others are families.

I hear Zaria talking to the bartender. I look over there and my world stops when the bartender nods and walks away.

She turns to a tall, beefy guy standing right next to her. He has short-clipped sandy brown hair and wears the most perfect tailored dark-grey suit I've ever seen. He looks way too dressed up to be on a cruise.

She looks up at him and a wicked light comes on in her dark eyes. She breaks into a smile and beams at him.

She nods down at the tumbler of brown liquid in his hand. "You're getting an early start, aren't you? Save it for tonight."

He turns his head just enough for me to see his profile. He has a powerful, chiseled jawline and incredible bright blue eyes.

"I'm flattered, but I'm happily married with children," he tells her. "I'm not a passenger and this is iced tea, not anything alcoholic. I work here. I'm the Chief of Security for this ship, so whatever it is you're looking for, I'm not interested. Have a pleasant voyage."

He downs his drink and walks away. Damn. What a boss.

Zaria's smile evaporates at his words. She stares with huge eyes as he walks out of the restaurant without a backward glance.

Her gaze pivots outward to the restaurant—and she sees me watching her.

That guy really knew how to shut her down. I need to take lessons from the guy.

I push back my chair and walk out, too. I make it halfway across the concourse before Zaria comes rushing after me. "Hey, wait! Reese! Wait!"

I keep walking until she gets right in front of me and blocks my way.

"What do you want from me?" I demand. "Did you really think you could flirt with someone right in front of me and get away with it? I've caught you cheating too many times before and you just keep going back to the gutter where you belong. I told you we're finished. I'm here to find someone else. When are you going to get that through your head?"

"Come on, Reese," she wheedles. "We're good for each other. We can work this out."

I snort at her. "Work what out, exactly—that you're a lying, cheating whore who can't keep her legs shut? You just flirted with a married man. Are there any depths you won't sink to?"

"Give me a break! I didn't know he was married!"

"And that somehow makes it okay when I'm sitting right there watching you?" I throw up my hands. "We aren't having this conversation. We're done. You go drag your ass through the streets as much as you want. I won't stand around to watch."

I walk around her to take off back toward the activity deck. She lunges for me and grabs my arm. "Reese—come on! Give me another chance!"

I yank my arm out of her grip. I might do it a little too hard, but I'm too steamed to care right now.

Fortunately for my sanity, she doesn't come after me again. There aren't enough bad words in the English language for me to insult her with.

I storm out onto the piazza, but I don't want to go out to the pool. I turn the other way. The safety briefing is just about to start.

The security guy stands next to Allie. She introduces him as Troy Nixon. The guy is a damn tank.

I have nothing but respect for the way he talked to Zaria. I need guys like him in my life.

I'm sure his wife is very happy. She probably knows he doesn't look sideways at other women when she isn't around, not even when he leaves on cruises for weeks at a time.

He surveys the crowd of passengers with eagle eyes through the whole briefing. I get the sense that he's evaluating us. He's deciding who is going to become a problem for him on this cruise and who will sail through with flying colors.

He has probably seen it all. Nothing can happen on this cruise that he can't handle.

His presence makes me feel better. I'm sure all the married men on board feel better with him around, too. No one has to worry about him making a move on anyone's wife or girlfriend.

I get busy looking around at the other passengers. I want to find someone on this cruise, at least for a brief fling. I need something to take my mind off how mad I am at Zaria.

As soon as we get home, I'm going to have to deal with all the ugly business of prying my life away from hers.

I have to move her out of my house—which will be a project unto itself. Then I'll have to inform all our friends and family what a skank she is and block all her friends from telling me how I should forgive her and take her back and what a prick I am for ruining her life. I don't need to hear that.

I don't see anyone interesting, but this is a pretty big crowd. I'm sure there are plenty of people on this cruise that I don't see right now.

The tour breaks up. I don't want to go back to the concourse. I don't want to run into Zaria.

That's going to become a problem because we're sharing the same suite. I only agreed to it to save money, but if I do find someone, I might have to get my own place. I *will* have to get my own place. There is no might about it.

I decide to skip the concourse and head out to the pool after all. I walk down the breezeway and spot a young woman sitting on a bench crying. I can't see her face because she buries it in her hands.

Her shoulders shake with sobs. Something about the way she's sitting here alone makes me stop and sit down next to her.

I don't really want to go to the pool. I don't want to be anywhere.

My relationship is over. Maybe I'm not the only person on this ship who is going through this right now. I can only hope.

This stranger looks nice in a pair of white shorts over slim, tanned legs, white sandals, and a floral-print T-shirt. She wears a light knit sweater tied around her waist.

The whole outfit shows off her figure. Wavy brown and tan high-lighted hair falls over her hands.

I don't know why I find her appealing except that she's the only person around here who doesn't act happy to be on this cruise.

"Are you okay?" I ask. "What's wrong?"

She bursts into full-throated sobs and wails out loud. She either doesn't see or doesn't care who might hear her.

"My marriage is over!" she howls. "The bastard cheated on me four times and then had the nerve to invite me on this cruise to try to work it out—as if I would ever take him back! And just a few minutes ago he suggested we have a couples swap so he can flaunt it right in front of me! Now I have to go home to a nasty divorce and listen to his family talk about how I was never good enough for him and all that crap! He ruined my life—and now I'm the one who has to clean up the mess!"

She breaks down bawling right there. Wow. That story sounds so much worse than mine.

It strikes a chord, though. I'm not the only one going through it. Thank Heaven for that.

I stare out at the waves and murmur under my breath. I might as well be talking to myself. "My girlfriend cheated on me, too."

She drops her hands and looks up at me. She's actually really pretty. Her deep, chestnut eyes swim in tears. Her face is blotchy and swollen from crying, but that can't hide her delicate features and sculpted nose and lips.

"Really?" she chokes.

I nod and find myself smiling at her. "I already told her it's over, but she insisted on inviting me on this cruise to try to work it out. She still says we're good for each other for some unknown reason—and I just caught her flirting with a guy right in front of me in the bar just now. She's a tramp and she'll never change. I already told her I came on this cruise to find someone else." I look away. "I just dread going home and facing the reality of breaking up with her. I wish I didn't have to go through all that."

She starts crying again, but at least she doesn't cover her face. Her mouth screws up the wrong way.

Her teary eyes dart out toward the ocean. "I know! I feel the same way—and now I'm sitting here crying when I should be enjoying this cruise! I want to appreciate all this beauty and luxury! I don't know when I'll get another chance to do this! I don't want to spend it dwelling on him!" She chokes once. "I wish I could hook up with someone on this cruise and show him what it feels like."

I get a sudden brainwave. I don't let myself think about it before I clasp her hand in mine. "I have an idea. We could do the couples swap—yours and mine. We could teach them both a lesson by hooking up with each other—you and me. What do you say?"

She blinks at me in stunned shock. "You mean—like—have sex... ..with each other?"

I burst out laughing. "Why not? It doesn't have to be forever. Just one night—just to show them both that we have other options."

She gapes at me. "You can do that?! I mean...I could do that?"

I can't stop smiling at her. She's gorgeous, genuine, and so open. I love the way she looks into my eyes and doesn't look away.

She doesn't try to hide the subtle nuances of her facial expressions. She shows her heart right there on her sleeve.

I take another chance and squeeze her hand. "I think you're really beautiful. I would love to hook up with you. We wouldn't be making any kind of lifetime commitment or anything. Just think about it. I can arrange for your husband to ask me and my girlfriend about doing a couples swap. Then you and I can go out for the night and you can come home in the morning and tell him you don't need him anymore because you found a real man."

She bursts out laughing even though she still has tears in her eyes. Holy crap, she is stunning when she laughs!

Light pours out of her eyes and face—and this is nothing like the wicked, sex-fueled light I see so often from Zaria.

I want this woman. I want her to be the one even if it's just for the duration of the cruise or even just for one night. She's the one I'm going to do it with. She's perfect.

I decide to back off and give her some space. I would really like to kiss her right now, but I settle for just squeezing her hand one more time.

"You think about it. I'll see you around the ship sometime." I stand up to walk away before I remember to hold out my hand. "I'm Reese, by the way. It was really nice to meet you."

She beams up at me through her tears and shakes my hand. She has small, soft, gentle hands. "I'm Selena. It was really nice to meet you, too. I hope I see you soon."

I smile back. I don't want to let go of her hand, but I do it anyway before I walk off toward the pool.

Chapter 3: Selena

I come downstairs from the suite I share with Landon. Thank the stars he wasn't there. I don't want to see him. I don't want to deal with him.

I spend an hour putting away my clothes and putting my personal items in the bathroom. The suite has two bedrooms so I don't have to share one with him.

I still haven't seen him since he dropped the bomb about the whole couples swap thing.

My stomach turns a somersault when I think about Reese. He's drop-dead gorgeous with curly, auburn hair, flashing golden eyes, and broad shoulders. He looks like he works out a lot.

He also has warm hands and a very soft touch. I love how he just sat down and started talking to me.

Knowing someone on this cruise is going through the same thing I am—it lifts a weight off my shoulders. I'm not the only person on the boat who isn't ecstatically in love with the person they're here with.

I can't wait to see Reese again. I don't know if I'm ready to just jump into bed with him, but I do want to see him again.

His attention—his suggestion—all of this is going to be the perfect antidote to all the Landon poison in my life. Reese is such a tonic to my broken heart.

I don't care if I ever see him again after the cruise ends. In fact, it would probably be better if I didn't.

I can have a good time with him, enjoy the attention he's giving me, get a jolt of confidence in my arm, and move on. I'll wait to look for something serious once I get back on dry land.

He probably lives on the other side of the country. I never have to worry about seeing him again anyway.

The boat departs from the pier while I'm still in the suite. I stand on the balcony and take a bunch of deep breaths of the salty air. I love the way it feels and smells. It blows all my problems away.

I watch the pier get farther and farther away. Then I turn my gaze out toward the ocean.

I stand out there for a long time and watch night settle over the water. It's so magnificently beautiful out here. Life is still sweet and good. I'll put Landon in my past and move on to bigger and better things.

I still haven't heard from him by the time I get dressed for dinner and go down to the concourse. I'm all ready to eat dinner by myself or maybe start looking around for Reese.

I pass one of the busier restaurants and spot Landon standing at the bar. I freeze in my tracks when I see him talking to Reese. Oh, my God! Are they really talking about the couples swap?

I didn't want to believe Reese when he said he wanted to do it. It sounds like some kind of wild porn fantasy—not something I could actually do in real life.

I study him and Landon standing side by side. Landon has dark hair, dark eyes, and he's taller than Reese.

Landon isn't as muscular, but that isn't what fascinates me about Reese. He has a sturdy, determined air that Landon lacks.

Reese strikes me as the kind of guy who sets himself on a path and doesn't waver.

He would be like that in a relationship, too. He sounded so hurt when he talked about his girlfriend cheating on him—and then flirting with a guy right in front of him. That has to hurt.

Reese wouldn't cheat. He feels so stung by her infidelity because he would never do that. He feels about his girlfriend the way I feel about Landon. Reese feels utterly betrayed.

He doesn't show it in his conversation with Landon. They talk easily and Reese laughs at Landon's jokes. They look like they're drinking together.

I don't want to see Landon. I do want to see Reese.

The wicked idea sneaks into my mind. I could hook up with Reese right in front of Landon's eyes. He wouldn't be able to stop me.

It would be the ultimate payback if he was the one who set me up with Reese. Reese is right. This is the best way to get back at both Landon and Reese's girlfriend, whoever she is.

The minute I think that, Reese points across the bar to a petite olive-skinned woman with long black hair. This isn't the woman Landon was checking out during the tour.

They look remarkably similar, though. Reese's girlfriend wears tight, short shorts and a tight, cropped top that shows off her midsection. The overhead lights sparkle on her rhinestone belly button ring.

Four other guys stand around hitting on her. She beams up at them basking in their attention. If I didn't know she had a boyfriend, I would think she was fishing to hook up with one of those guys tonight.

She doesn't have a boyfriend. Reese already split up with her. He's a free agent and so is she.

Landon's eyes widen when he sees her. He turns away with an effort and nods at Reese. They're making the deal of a lifetime.

That's my cue to walk into the restaurant. I'm wearing a short, floral summer dress with tightly sheered elastic around the waist, hips, and bust. The ruffled sleeves connect to the dress under my armpits and leave my chest exposed without too much cleavage.

Landon spots me and waves. I point to one of the tables and sit down.

He goes back to talking to Reese and then points me out. Reese turns around like he's seeing me for the first time.

Our eyes meet across the crowded restaurant. I want to do it with him. I want him to be the one. He's perfect. Landon has no idea what he's getting himself into.

Reese only looks at me for a minute and turns back to nod at Landon. Landon doesn't notice the look passing between me and Reese. Landon is completely oblivious.

The waiter comes over and I order a drink and my meal. Landon can take care of himself. I don't pay more attention to anything going on between Landon and Reese.

The food and my drink come before Landon finishes talking to Reese. Reese leaves and Landon crosses the restaurant to my table.

He kisses me on the cheek before he collapses into the seat with a heavy sigh. "Well, it's all set up! That guy I was just talking to is down for the couples swap. He's certain his girlfriend is up for it, too. He just has to talk to her and he'll text me tonight if it's all on."

I put a bite of my mashed potatoes in my mouth and start chewing. I can already see where this is going.

He puts his arm behind my back, leans in, and murmurs in my ear. "You know you're going to love it. This is so exciting! I can't wait to start this new chapter of our relationship."

He kisses me again—on the neck this time. He kisses under my ear and burrows in.

I pretend not to notice and start cutting up my steak. I put a piece of that in my mouth next.

I'm not sure if Landon senses that I'm not responding. He sits up straight and beams down into my eyes. "Come on. Tell me you're happy about this whole couples swap. Did you see the guy? He isn't bad-looking, don't you think?"

I rest my forearms on the table and face him. "I'm going to go through with this couples swap thing....."

He bursts into a huge grin. "Great! I can't wait for you to meet him!"

"I just want you to know ahead of time that we're over. We don't have a relationship and we aren't starting a new chapter. We're finished. Done. Kaput. I'm telling you now so you won't come back and accuse me of cheating later."

"I wouldn't do that!" he exclaims. "This is going to be good for us! You'll see."

"There is no us, Landon. I'm splitting up with you. If you want to go sleep with someone else, go right ahead. You're free. You're single, so go mingle. I won't try to stop you."

"Come on! Don't be like that. Just meet them. You'll see I'm right."

I bend over my plate and go back to eating. "Don't say I didn't warn you."

Chapter 4: Reese

I unlock the door to the suite, step inside, and see Zaria sitting on the couch in the living room.

She's wearing one of the cruise line's fluffy white bathrobes and she has her hair twisted up in a bun. She dresses like this and puts her hair up when she gets ready to go to bed.

She jumps up when I walk in. "Where have you been?!" she demands. "I've been looking for you for hours!"

"I was right there in the same restaurant with you." I sit down in the armchair across from her. "I'm surprised you didn't see me. I could see you the whole time."

She looks away. She didn't see me because she had her head three feet up some other guys' asses the whole evening.

I saw plenty of her hitting on them and flaunting her body in front of their drooling mouths. She's such an attention addict. I should have seen it a long time ago.

Never mind. It's over now.

She's busy filing her toenails. A bottle of nail polish sits on the coffee table in front of her. Of course she has to look her best for when some dude picks her up in a bar downstairs.

I take the bull by the horns. "You probably didn't see the guy I was talking to at the bar......"

She doesn't look up. She keeps filing. "No, I didn't see any-thing—and I didn't know you were there, so I wouldn't have seen who you were talking to."

"He wants to have a couples swap between us and him and his wife."

Her head shoots up and she stares at me. "You mean.....?"

"I mean you would hook up with him and I would hook up with his wife. I pointed you out to him in the bar and he pointed out his wife." I pull out my phone and show her a picture of Landon Neise.

Her eyes light up when she sees him. She doesn't even think she might be offending me by finding him attractive. What a tramp.

"He's cute!" She hands back the phone and grins at me. "Do you like his wife?"

I nod slowly. I can't smile. I knew she would get excited about this. "She's really sweet and pretty. He invited us to have dinner with them tomorrow night—just to get to know each other."

"Great!" She beams at me. "It sounds fun!"

"If it happens, it would happen on Thursday—three days from now—day after day after tomorrow."

She laughs, puts down her nail file, and comes over to my chair.

She sits down on my lap, puts her arm around my neck, and nuzzles into my neck. "This is going to be really good for us! It's time we got out there and saw what else was available. It will bring us closer together."

I don't answer. I knew she would see this as an opening for us to get back together—or not break up in the first place.

I wait an appropriate amount of time before I gently push her off my lap. "I'm tired. I'm gonna go to sleep. I'll see you in the morning."

I see at a glance that she's set up all her stuff in one of the suite bedrooms off the living room. I get my suitcase, wheel it into the other bedroom, and shut the door before she has a chance to protest.

I make sure to lock the door from the inside. I don't want her to get any crazy ideas about sneaking into my bed in the middle of the night.

I crash hard and spend the day avoiding Zaria. She makes it easy because she spends all her time on the concourse.

The one time I do see her, I spot her in the casino getting other guys to pay for her gambling. They also buy her drinks. I recognize the signs of early intoxication.

I hope she's sober enough to see straight when the time comes for us to meet up with Landon and Selena.

I see both of them at different times, but they aren't together and I don't talk to either of them. I also avoid Selena. I want to preserve the illusion that I don't know her, have never met her, and that I'll be meeting her for the first time tonight at dinner.

I start to get excited by the time I make my way back to the suite to change for dinner. Zaria is already there.

She puts on a tight-fitting white sequined dress with a low-cut top, spaghetti straps, and a stretchy fabric that shows off every curve.

Her stacked chest practically falls out the top. Her wide hips and round ass would turn any guy's head, but only if he wants to smash her and go home that same night.

She puts on an unbelievable amount of makeup considering she's only supposed to be meeting one guy. She also wears knock-me-over heels that make her look even more like a streetwalker.

I'm sure Landon will love her. She's exactly the kind of woman a man like him would go for.

I put on a nice suit. I make sure I look good for Selena. I need to make a good impression on her.

She saw me in shorts, tennis shoes, and a short-sleeved shirt that first time. I need to change that so she sees me as a much classier guy than her sleaze husband.

Zaria won't stop blushing when she takes my arm and I escort her downstairs. We meet up with Landon and Selena in a different restaurant.

This one is quieter and more expensive. Zaria looks way out of place, but Selena looks absolutely mouth-watering.

She wears another thigh-length red dress, but this one is simple with a square-cut top and no frills. She wears large gold hoop earrings, a simple, thin gold chain around her neck, and no other jewelry.

I notice right away that she isn't wearing her wedding band anymore. Does Landon even notice?

He doesn't because he can't put his tongue back in his mouth when he sees Zaria. He's so busy gushing over how gorgeous she is that he doesn't see Selena stand up to greet me.

She blushes so beautifully when she smiles at me, shakes my hand, and tells me that it's nice to meet me. I give her a quick hug, kiss her on the cheek, and she laughs again.

She looks so much more stunning, now that she isn't crying. She radiates simple elegance. She isn't trampy or ostentatious. Her pure beauty shines through.

I sit down next to her and Zaria sits down next to Landon. Landon and Zaria start talking to each other. That leaves me to talk to Selena.

"How are you doing?" I ask.

She won't stop blushing and beaming at me. Holy crap, I have to calm down!

"I'm really good!" I love seeing her color with nervous excitement. "How are you?"

"I'm great. It's really great to see you again. I'm surprised you agreed to this whole swap idea."

She bursts out in excited laughter. "It's like you said. It will be the best way to get the point across. Did you actually suggest it to him?"

"I said both Zaria and I were here to enjoy ourselves and see what kind of trouble we could get ourselves into—which is the truth in a strange kind of way. He got all interested and said you two were here to do the same thing."

She groans and rolls her eyes. "He is, for certain."

I throw caution to the wind and extend my hand between our chairs to take hers. "We won't get into trouble, but I am definitely looking forward to this. You're just what the doctor ordered."

She colors again, but she won't stop smiling. She looks me straight in the eyes and doesn't look away when she squeezes my hand back. "I feel the same way. I feel like meeting you is going to be the best thing for me."

"So tell me more about yourself—apart from anything related to your marriage. What do you do for work?"

"I'm an artist."

My eyebrows fly up. "Really? Wow! So do you do showings and stuff like that? Do you actually make a living at that?"

"Oh, no, not like that!" She laughs again. Her energy gives me the chills. "I work for an agency doing illustrations for children's books. I get commissions so I always have regular work."

"That's amazing. Did you go to school for that?"

She nods. I find myself getting hypnotized by the color glowing off her cheeks and in her eyes. She radiates beauty that casts the rest of the room in shadow.

The energy flowing into my hand from hers makes me weak in the knees. I can't wait to get my hands on her, but I don't just want to knock her down, steamroll over her, and leave in the morning like a thief in the night.

I want to romance her. I want to take her out and let the whole world see me getting closer to her. I want to feel her beautiful magnetic energy right next to me and see her looking into my eyes exactly the way she's looking into my eyes right now.

I have to concentrate to pay attention what she's telling me about how she went to art school and one of her instructors recommended her to the agency she currently works for.

That's when I become aware that Landon and Zaria aren't talking to each other anymore. He sits in his chair glaring at me while I hold his wife's hand.

Maybe once a long time ago she looked at him the way she's looking at me right now. He's a friggin' idiot ever to devalue a woman like this.

I would never let her look away from me if she was my woman. I would do absolutely anything to get her to look at me like this all the time.

She'll never look at that fool like this again. Maybe now he'll realize what a prize he threw away by being a man whore and a hound.

Selena is in the middle of telling me how she got her start at the agency when Landon skids his chair back, stands up, and grabs Selena by her other hand.

"Come on, Selena," he snaps. "It's getting late. It's time to go back to the suite."

"Hey!" she exclaims. "We just got here!"

"Let's go!" he barks and pulls her away from the table.

Her hand slips out of mine, but her skin leaves an indelible mark on me. I find myself rubbing my fingers together so I can feel the sensation a little longer.

He drags her out of the restaurant, but they only get a few yards down the concourse before she pulls away from him and they start arguing.

"I didn't bring you here to flirt with the guy right in front of me!" Landon snaps.

"No, you brought me here so some stranger could fuck me," she fires back. "This whole couples swap was your idea, remember? Don't you dare start acting jealous when you're the one who has been sleeping around—and don't you dare try to pretend that you weren't planning to do it with Zaria."

"That isn't the point!" Landon counters. "We're here to fix our relationship—not so you can run off with another guy."

"You're here to run off with another girl! Don't think I haven't seen you eyeing every other woman on the boat. Anyway, we aren't here to fix our relationship because we have no relationship! I told you that yesterday. We're finished. Get that through your head. What I do is none of your business anymore. Besides, you can't back out of it because you already set the day and time with Reese. You made your bed. Now you have to lie in it."

She storms off. He stays there floundering in confusion for a minute before he hurries after her.

Zaria is too busy talking to the waiter to overhear Landon's and Selena's conversation.

I get a sadistic thrill seeing Landon in turmoil over the situation. This is working out so much better than I planned.

Chapter 5: Selena

I smooth down the sides of my black dress. It's tight around the waist with ruffles just above my knees and a sweetheart neckline.

I turn sideways to make sure I look all right from every angle. Then I step closer to the mirror to make sure my makeup looks right.

Landon paces the room behind me. "You can't go through with this, baby. I love you. We can work this out."

"Don't you ever call me that again, you lying, scumbag cheater," I mutter under my breath without turning around. "You're the one who set this up with Reese. You're the one who told me this would bring us closer together and breathe new life into our relationship. You're only getting cold feet now because you see that I'm attracted to Reese. I hope you're happy because you got exactly what you asked for."

He comes up behind me. "I'll do better. I promise I won't sleep around anymore."

I gasp in exasperation and walk away from him to put my phone and compact mirror in my purse. "Do you even know how many times you've already said that? You are so pathetic, Landon. Get a new line. Your old lies are really wearing thin."

He dogs my footsteps around the suit while I make one last check of my hair and adjust the heel of one of my shoes.

"What will it take?" he practically begs. "I'll do anything."

"You said that when we first got married, but apparently, you'll do anything other than be faithful. I would have stayed with you forever. I stayed loyal to you all these years. You would be married to me right now if you only did what you said you were going to do from the beginning. There is nothing you can do because you already did it." I raise my left hand so he can see that I'm not wearing my wedding band anymore. "See? You did this—not me."

I go through the room making sure I have my key to the suite and everything else I might need, including my wallet.

He stops across the room watching me put on the last of my jewelry. "If you do this, we're finished. There's no coming back from this. If you go out with him, I won't be able to take you back. I could never look at you the same way again if you gave yourself to another man."

I snort in his general direction. "Now you know how I feel. You're tainted by God only knows how many other women—but that doesn't matter because I already split up with you. I've been single for three days."

"You can't do this to me!" His voice starts to rise. "You can't betray me like this! I would never do anything like this to you!"

"You already did, Landon! You already cheated four times—and those are only the times I know about! You know you've done it more than that! Don't start playing holier than thou!"

"I'm talking about Zaria! I'm not going out to hook up with her!"

"Do you think I give a crap about Zaria?! Go fuck the shit out of Zaria for all I care! You are the one who destroyed our marriage, Landon. You destroyed it a long time ago!" My hand flies to my head. "Oh, my God! Why do I even bother to argue with you about it? Do you want to know the craziest part of all of this? I've been single for years! We haven't been married for years if we ever were! Do you understand that now? You left me years ago so you could go roll in the hay with every skank that walks the streets. Well, now you can. No one is stopping you. We aren't married anymore. You're a free man, so you have nothing to say about what I do. I really hope you do sleep with Zaria. She looks like she's perfect for you."

"How can you be so cruel?!" he counters. "I would never sleep with her."

I groan. "No, you would just sleep with any other woman who will have you. I wish you all the best of luck in the world with that. I hope you live to a nice ripe old age alone after you're too wrinkled and shriveled to get any woman to look sideways at you."

He opens his mouth to argue back, but right then, we hear a knock on the door. Landon and I both freeze staring at each other.

I recover first and turn to go over there to open it. He dives into my path and puts his arm out in front of me. "Don't do this, Selena."

"You did it, you stupid piece of shit," I snarl. "Now get the hell out of my way before I call security."

He gapes at me in horror and backs off. I open the door and turn bright red when I see Reese standing there in a magnificent suit. He looks like a million bucks.

"Hi!" I gasp.

He smiles at me and bites back a grin when he says, "Hi."

His sharp golden eyes dart sideways to Landon standing behind me. Reese's expression goes through another series of transformations when he sees Landon.

A mixture of cruel triumph, contempt, and pity struggle in Reese's features before he bites back another smirk.

He glances at me. "Are you ready to go?"

"Yeah!" I walk out of the suite and he takes my hand.

"Don't worry, man!" Reese calls over my shoulder. "I'll take good care of her!"

He pulls the door shut behind me so Landon doesn't get a chance to answer.

Reese lets his grin break all the way out once we're alone in the corridor. He pulls my hand through the corner of his elbow. "Are you okay?" he breathes.

"Yeah!" I pant. "I'm sorry if you overheard anything."

"I overheard a lot of it. I was standing outside during almost the entire argument." He presses my hand. "You did great."

I turn bright red again. "I'm sorry you had to hear any of it. I can't believe he's being such a drip about it when he was the one who came up with the idea." I shake those thoughts out of my head. "I don't want to spend our time together talking about that."

"I like talking about it with you. It makes me feel like I'm not the only one going through this."

I look up to find his eyes glowing down at me. He looks so much more intense, now that we're alone.

"How is Zaria about the whole thing?" I ask.

"Oh, she's thrilled about it. She just spent two hours getting ready to go out with Landon. She thinks this is the best thing ever."

My jaw drops. "Really? You didn't tell her....like that it's over?"

"Oh, I've told her dozens of times. She thinks I'm giving her another chance with this couples swap. I told her to have a good time."

I shake my head and look away. "That's incredible. I could never do something like that."

"I really hope they hook up with each other. You're right about them. They deserve each other."

I squirm in my skin. "Can we stop talking about this? I don't want to talk about it anymore."

"Okay. I really enjoyed hearing about your work last night. It's a shame Landon cut us off before I got a chance to find out more about you."

I blush and smile. "I would really like to get to know you better, too."

"Let's go down to the concourse and have dinner together. We can take it from there."

I find myself laughing. "You mean....we aren't going to hook up right here and now?"

He makes a face. "Landon and Zaria might do it that way, but I don't want to. I want to take you out and see if we have any chemistry."

I try to look away, but his eyes won't let me. "I think we both already know we have chemistry."

"We don't have to do anything. The plan between me and Landon was for both of us to rent separate rooms for tonight. I don't know where he'll be taking Zaria and he doesn't know where I'll be taking you—if we decide to go through with this, of course. That way, no one can interrupt the other couple while anything is going on."

I smack my lips in exasperation. "He really thinks of everything, doesn't he?"

"Apparently not." We step into the elevator and he presses the button for the concourse.

"So what do you do for work?" I ask.

"I'm a sales rep for a major motorcycle brand. I go around coordinating with all the showrooms, retailers, and repair shops arranging their new shipments, parts orders, and everything else they need."

My eyes fly open. "Wow. A motorcycle guy. I never would have guessed after the way you....." My gaze darts down to his suit. He looks about as far from a motorcycle guy as I've ever seen.

"It's a great job and I love it. I spend most of my time standing around shooting the breeze with other motorcycle guys talking about motorcycles. We all know a vast amount of totally useless information about every make and model of motorcycle on the market, which parts go with which models for which purposes, and everything else no one else in the world is interested in. It's a great job."

I laugh. "It sounds like you found your calling in life."

"I did. It's perfect for me. I get to spend all my time talking, thinking, and interacting with people about my passion—and I get paid for it. It doesn't get any better than that."

I find myself beaming at him. "It sounds like my job."

"Yeah, I was thinking the same thing."

The elevator opens on the concourse. Reese and I step outside, but he stops me there before we walk away.

He uses my hand to pull me close—close enough to kiss—but he doesn't kiss me. His eyes drift down to my mouth, then back to my eyes, and to my hair and all my other features.

"I want tonight to be about us, too," he murmurs. "I think you're amazing. I want tonight to be about us seeing if we have something apart from Landon and Zaria. I want you to know I wouldn't be going out with you at all if I didn't see something in you—something I want to get close to. I don't want this to be about just sex."

I can't speak above a whisper. His presence captivates me as never before. "I want that, too," I breathe. "I see the same thing in you. I want this to be about us—not them."

He barely smiles. "Come on. Let's go."

Chapter 6: Reese

I pull out Selena's chair for her in a swanky restaurant on the top level of the concourse. This is the nicest, most exclusive, most expensive restaurant on the boat.

The fact that it's so exclusive and expensive means it's also the quietest restaurant on the boat. Only two other couples are in here.

One is an older couple sitting in a corner and tapping their champagne flutes together. I catch Selena watching them. "They look like they really know how to go the distance with each other, don't they?" she remarks.

"Yeah." I stretch my hand across the table. "And so do we."

She blushes again and turns to face me. "Why do I feel so comfortable around you?"

"Maybe it was meant to be. You're so different from Zaria."

"Do you ever feel stupid for getting together with someone so unsuitable?" she asks. "I can't help but kick myself for believing his lies."

"You can't blame yourself for what he did. He's a scumbag. You were loyal and you had every reason to believe he meant it when he made his vows."

"I didn't have to stay with him after the first time.....or the second time....or the third time. I'm a sucker."

I look away. "Yeah. I guess I'm a sucker that way, too."

She gets my attention by squeezing my hand. "We can be suckers together."

My attention snaps back to her in a heartbeat. "I would be very happy to be a sucker for you."

"As long as I can be a sucker for you," she replies and bestows another beaming smile on me.

My heart flips when she smiles like that, but just then, the waiter comes. We order our food and drinks.

We rejoin hands the minute he leaves. I can't stop staring at her across the table.

A moment of meaningful silence falls over me when our eyes meet. Neither of us says anything for what seems like a long time.

I would be perfectly content to sit here staring into her eyes for the rest of the night. I don't even feel the need to take her back to the room I rented for tonight. This is so much better.

I really feel something growing between us.

She startles out of her trance. "So tell me more. How did you wind up selling motorcycle parts?"

"I was working in sales in another industry and I hated it. I was already looking for another job and telling myself I would never do sales again as long as I lived."

"What did you think you wanted to do instead?"

"I thought I might become a plumber."

She explodes in laughter. Her eyes twinkle and her cheeks flush. I love making her laugh.

"I can just see you bending over with your pants around your ankles and some harried housewife checking you out from behind." She covers her mouth. "I am never going to let you live that down."

I smile at her. "That's right. Laugh it up."

"Sorry." She chokes down laughter and fails. "So what happened? How did you make the switch?"

"I was in a motorcycle shop fantasizing about all the bikes I would buy just as soon as I won the lottery. I noticed a sign on the shop wall advertising for a sales position. I figured it couldn't possibly be worse than the job I had then. I figured I would still hate sales but at least I would be selling something I was interested in and talking to people about our shared passion. The rest is history."

She rests her chin in her hand and gazes at me across the table. "Wow. That sounds like a fairy-tale ending."

"It was. That's actually how I met Zaria."

Her eyes snap wide open. "It is?"

"I met her at a motorcycle rally where I was manning the booth for the company I work for now. I thought she was there because she was really interested in motorcycles. I know now that she only went there to hook up with guys."

She clucks her tongue and shakes her head. "It must be terrible to think that about someone you used to love."

"You must have a story like that about Landon. How did it happen for you?"

She winces. "I guess we're talking about this after all."

"We're getting to know each other. I want to know about your past. Don't worry. It doesn't make me think any less of you."

She makes a few more faces before she spills the story. "We met in college. We were both majoring in art, but he switched to finance after two years. We shared a lot of the same classes in those early days. That's how we met."

"So is he an artist, too?"

She shrugs. "It isn't a lifetime project for him. It was more of a hobby, I think. Anyway, when I met him, he was just a young guy going to classes, doing his homework, and learning how to survive on his own for the first time. He came across as a wholesome, introverted, thoughtful, sensitive kind of guy—which I guess he was. He was all of those things—and we were both young, innocent, and idealistic."

"So how did it all change?"

She looks off into the distance thinking about her past memories. "I didn't find out until about five years ago that he had an ongoing affair with another woman from his work. They had been meeting on their lunch breaks and hooking up after executive meetings that ran outside of their daily schedule. He always had a cover story or he did it during work time so I wouldn't see anything suspicious. He kept coming home at the same time every night and going through the same routine for over a year before I found out."

"Wow," I breathe. "A whole year. I don't think Zaria can go more than a week with the same person."

"I found out purely by chance. I was doing a contract with the agency, and in the middle of the workday, I got a call from my sister that one of her sons broke his arm at school. She asked me to pick up her younger son from daycare because she couldn't leave the hospital just yet. I drove into town and went to the hospital to meet my sister so I could get the younger boy's car seat out of my sister's car so I could drive my nephew safely. I was putting the car seat in the car when I spotted Landon and this woman across the street. They were leaning against the wall kissing, making out, and groping each other all over. She had her hand down his pants and he was grabbing both her breasts through her shirt. He had her pinned to the wall and kept riding his hips between her legs while they stuck their tongues down each other's throats."

"So what did you do?" I ask.

"I was too stunned to do anything at first. I just stared at them. Then I realized what was happening, so I took a picture of them on my phone and kept on going with the business of picking up my nephew. I confronted Landon when he came home and the whole story blew up."

"How did he justify it?"

"He said it was a mistake—that it happened on the spur of the moment and in a moment of weakness and a bunch of other nonsense. Then, later, after I questioned him some more, he let it slip that the first time happened over a year earlier and he'd been having these moments of weakness multiple times a week ever since."

I shake my head. "That is terrible. I'm so sorry."

"He begged forgiveness, said it wouldn't happen again, and promised to break it off with her immediately."

"Did he?"

"Oh, yeah! I checked up on him. He never did it with her again. A week later, I got an irate visit from her. She came to my house and interrupted me in the middle of work to tell me that he promised to leave me so he could marry her. She even had an engagement ring, but he ended it right after I busted him."

"So what happened after that? When did he do it the next time?"

"I didn't find out about it until six months later, but he started up with someone else four months after that initial confrontation. I was much more alert to the signs, so I caught him sooner. The first woman also made an enormous stink around the office and told everyone what was going on, so he didn't dare to get involved with anyone from work again. He had to find someone outside of work, which made him easier to catch."

"How did you catch him that time?"

"He hooked up with a desperate, lonely housewife who was home alone with her one-year-old baby all day long. Landon used to go over there on his lunch break and bang her while the kid was taking a nap."

I wince. "Classy."

She snorts. "That's putting it mildly. The woman's husband came home from work early one day and caught them in the act. He called me and told me."

"That sounds like how I first found out about Zaria," I tell her.

She jolts upright. "Really? What happened?"

"She hooked up with a guy in a bar. They did it for like ten seconds in the men's bathroom."

She snorts. "Classy."

"Sometimes I think she enjoys the dirty, filthy, crude aspect of it. She gets off on how trashy she can make it. Anyway, the guy's best friend saw them together and the best friend told me. It turns out he works as a mechanic in one of the bike shops I supply, so he knew me."

"That's cool that he had your back like that."

"As soon as he told me, it was like the floodgates opened and all the other stories started coming out of the woodwork. As soon as I opened my eyes, I saw it everywhere."

"How many times did she do it?"

"I only found out about five of them, but I'm certain she was doing it all the time. She doesn't stick with one person the way Landon does. She's a wham, bam, thank you ma'am type of girl."

Selena giggles, but right then, the waiter comes with our food. She keeps smirking at me across the table while we eat.

"So are you going to be a wham, bam, thank you ma'am type of girl for me?" I ask.

She blushes and pretends to hide it by sipping her drink. "Let's see how tonight goes before we decide on that. You might decide you don't even like me."

"Oh, I like you," I tell her. "I like you a lot."

She blushes again. "I like you, too."

Chapter 7: Selena

Reese puts his arm behind my waist and pulls me against him as we lean against the railing out on the deck of the *Electric Emerald*.

The moon casts a perfectly straight path of silver brilliance over the smooth ocean surface.

The cool wind bites through my thin, short dress, but heat radiates into me through Reese's clothes. He throbs with heat like a furnace.

I shiver with excitement when he holds me this close. We just spent a wonderful evening having dinner and talking about every aspect of our lives.

Now we're standing on the deck in the moonlight. This couldn't be more romantic if someone painted a picture of it.

"Do you still like me?" he murmurs in my ear.

"Yes," I murmur back. "Do you still like me?"

"Even more than before." He leans in and nuzzles his face against my hair. "You're perfect in every way."

I don't know what to say, so I keep gazing out at the ocean. We're supposed to go to some private room and hook up after this.

The thought turns me on. Am I being trashy like Zaria? I don't want to be, but I still want to do it with Reese.

He pushes me up just enough to turn me around to face him. His eyes gleam with hidden meaning.

"I meant what I said before," he tells me. "This is about us. It isn't about revenge or anything like that. I don't want us to do it if it isn't real between us—as if neither of us was getting out of another relationship."

"I feel the same way. I wouldn't do it if I didn't feel that for you."

He raises his hand, lays it against my cheek, and peers even deeper into my eyes if that's possible. "I see unlimited possibilities with you. I don't even feel like I'm getting out of another relationship. I feel like you and I are starting up fresh with no other attachments on either side."

I find myself trying to look away. "There's just one thing."

"What?" he breathes. "Tell me anything. I need to know what's going on with you."

"I'm still married," I blurt out. "I don't want you to think I'm not serious about leaving Landon....but I'll probably still be married for a while—at least until I get back home and deal with all the paperwork and everything."

"I know that. I know you're still married. I just want to know your feelings for me are real and you aren't just doing this to get back at him."

"No!!" I exclaim. "Not at all! I wouldn't do that! I mean, I wouldn't have gone out with you at all if you didn't suggest it, but now that I am.....I feel the same way you do—like nothing else ever happened before and this is all brand new."

He takes his hand down and smiles. "That's good. I'm glad we both see it that way."

I expect him to turn away and he does. I do, too. I turn back to looking at the moon, but when I do, he pulls me against him from behind. He eases me down on top of him, wraps his arms around me, and leans my weight against him.

This feels so easy—so right. I don't have to make this something it isn't. I don't have to argue and cajole to get him to show me that he wants to be with me.

I don't have to wonder if he's thinking about someone else. When was the last time I felt that with anyone?

I can't remember the last time I trusted Landon like this. I'm not even sure I ever did.

Reese rests his mouth and face against the back of my hair. He doesn't try to pressure me into doing anything else.

I don't have to do it with him. I know that now. I don't have to do anything.

He would wait as long as I need him to. He would wait forever if I asked him to.

I sink into the blissful rightness of this moment. I understand and feel the same way now. Nothing exists but this moment. Nothing exists but us.

I can almost believe that we both came on board alone, met up, and fell into this effortless connection with each other. Not even the couples swap exists anymore.

My relationship with Landon and all the sickening years I spent with him—they all feel like a story I once heard. It sounds like something that happened to someone else.

I've been with Reese all this time. I've been happily married to him. No one ever cheated on me—certainly not the way Landon did.

Reese doesn't move. He could stay like that all night if I wanted him to. He'll never take the next step. He'll never be the one to suggest that we go back to the room and....do whatever.

He'll wait for me to say so. He'll wait until I tell him I'm ready.

I pull out of his arms, turn around, and face him. His eyes glow in the moonlight. He's happy like this. He doesn't need anything else.

It's time. I know it. I lean in and kiss him. He kisses me back. That kiss gets deeper, warmer, more succulent, more passionate.

He wraps his arms around my waist, lifts me against him, and sways me back and forth while we kiss.

He sets me on my feet, sweeps his hand up to the back of my neck, and steers my mouth deeper into his.

I get lost in the hot, sultry passion of kissing him. I want him. I want him to take me back to the secret room where Landon will never find us.

I want to do all those forbidden things with Reese. I want to find out all the secrets that might lie between us. I want to explore every hidden corner of his being—and I want to do it far away from Landon and all other prying eyes.

I pull out of Reese's arms and straighten up. My mind still buzzes with desire and excitement. I clasp both his hands and tell him, "I'm ready."

His eyes widen. He really didn't expect that. "Are you sure? I don't want you to feel any pressure."

"I don't. I want to."

He studies me for a minute with his eyebrows raised. Then he shrugs. "Okay. Your wish is my command."

I giggle. I'm so excited and nervous all at the same time.

He takes my hand and leads me back down the piazza to the elevators. We stand there smirking at each other while we wait for the elevator to come.

A few other couples show up to go upstairs to their suites. I get really nervous when I realize I'm about to go cheat on my husband with another man. I'm standing here holding another man's hand while I'm still married to my husband.

I'm not married to Landon anymore. It's over. It's his problem if he's too delusional to face reality.

He'll never face reality. He'll keep pulling the wool over his own eyes until I finally divorce him and get with someone else.

I catch Reese glancing at me. Does he feel any hesitation about sleeping with someone other than Zaria? He doesn't show it, but he can't show it with all these other people around.

The elevator doors open. Everyone waiting steps on board the elevator. Then we all have to adjust our positions to make space for each other.

Reese and I wind up in the very back. I expect him to stand perfectly straight during the ride upstairs.

He leans against the wall, pulls me in front of him, and wraps his arms around me again to pull me against him.

He buries his face in my neck, and this time, he grinds his hips into my ass from behind. He's so unbelievably hard that I almost gasp out in ragged desire.

That hardness tells me in no uncertain terms what he wants to do with me. We aren't going upstairs to make out.

He doesn't touch me in any other way. Everyone can see him holding me, but no one knows how much he's arousing my hidden fantasies. I've been fantasizing about him non-stop since I met him.

The elevator doors pling again and open on a different deck of passenger suites. Half the people in the elevator get out. Then the same thing happens at the next deck.

There's only one more couple in the elevator with us. Reese pushes me up to stand on my own two feet. He eases off the wall and takes my hand like he never did anything to me.

My flesh aches between my legs. I want him so bad. I want him to do everything with me and to me. I want his body on me and mine on his.

The elevator dings at the next level. This is the highest deck of the ship—the same deck where I share a suite with Landon.

The other couple gets out. Reese takes my hand and leads me off the elevator. We walk down the corridor, past the suite I share with Landon, and farther toward the other end of the ship.

I find myself looking around at everything even though the corridor looks identical here.

We turn a corner and Reese reacts before I realize what's happening. He turns in my direction, pushes me against the wall, and starts kissing me again.

He pulls off in a second, but he doesn't lift his weight off me. He rests one arm against the wall above my head and stares deeply into my eyes while he grinds his body into me all the way down to my hips.

His hardness digs into me through my dress and makes me moan, but I can't shut my eyes. I have no choice but to stare all the way into his soul while he mesmerizes me to the stars.

His body breathes with so much tightly wound energy. My flesh sizzles with desire for him. I imagine him on top of me grinding his hips into me just like this.

His eyes hold me spellbound. His features go hard as granite when he watches me moan and whimper in front of him.

I don't even care that he's seeing me so ragged and vulnerable for him. I want him to. I want him to see how much I ache for him. I want him to see what I'll look like once he gets me into that room.

We could stand here forever. Standing here feeling his body on top of me feels like we're already doing it. We share that without even taking our clothes off. It's already over. We're already bonded to each other for all time in that way.

I don't know the moment it happens. Nothing changes between us, but he pulls off, takes my hand, and keeps going as if we never shared that moment at all.

We did share it. It happened and nothing can ever undo it.

If I go back to Landon right now, I can honestly say I shared the greatest night of passionate carnal bliss with Reese.

He stops in front of another suite. It looks like all the others. He uses another key card to unlock the door and leads me into a different suite. It's set up exactly the same as all the others.

He doesn't turn on the light. The moon glistens on the ocean outside balcony windows. That light casts a silver sheen through the room and creates a ghostly, romantic atmosphere.

I stroll to the balcony overlooking the ocean. Reese shuts the suite door behind me. He doesn't follow me.

I gaze out at the moon. The beauty of the ocean calms my nerves. The moon and the glistening water tell me the same thing. This is right. I'm where I'm supposed to be.

I turn around and see Reese sitting on one of the stools at the kitchen counter. He watches me from a distance.

I smile at him, but he doesn't smile back. Is he wondering if I'll go through with this, now that I'm actually in the room with him?

I've never been more certain of anything in my life. This suite—it somehow means what my suite with Landon was supposed to mean.

I was supposed to come on this cruise with the man who means the world to me—the man I never have to question—the man who is always there for me. Now I *am* on the cruise with that man. He sits right there across the room from me.

I walk over to him. He rests his hands on my waist and draws me between his knees as I slip my arms around his neck.

I fall into his kiss as magically as if it was meant to be—because it was.

It must have been Fate that made him sit down next to me on that bench. This cruise is turning out to be as magical, as romantic, and as fated as I ever dreamed—because of him.

Chapter 8: Reese

Selena rocks in my arms when I kiss her. She arches her body into me when I pull her toward me. She never holds herself back from me.

Her lips warm my whole face. That heat spreads to my heart and soul. I've never kissed a woman as open and giving as she is. Kissing her cracks my heart in half with so much emotion.

I almost feel like I love her and I haven't even spent the night with her. I don't have to spend the night with her. I already know she's the one I want to be with.

If we go through with tonight or not—it doesn't matter anymore. She's the reason I came on this cruise. She's the only reason I'm even here right now.

Her body tenses every time I do anything to her. I almost hesitate to go there with her. It could be more than I can reasonably handle, but I'm going there anyway.

I want so much more from her than just sex. I want to see that look in her eyes—the look she gave me at dinner that night—the smoking hot look of pure surrender she gave me in the hall just now—all the subtle looks in her eyes that let me see straight through her to the pure soul inside.

She's too far away from me even here. I scoop her up under her armpits and lift her onto my lap on the stool. She responds perfectly and spreads her legs to straddle me.

Her dress covers her down to her thighs. I don't need to see anything more.

Her body undulates in my hands. She gasps out loud and her eyes float half shut when she rides down on my hard package. Oh, my God! She is so unbelievably beautiful when she pants like that!

I kiss her, and when I pull off, her eyes float open to meet mine.

I stare as deeply into her as I want to. I can't get enough of watching her rock herself into oblivion.

I stroke my fingertips through her hair and down her neck. She clenches her hands on my shoulders to steady herself and hold back torrential passion.

I grab her waist, her hips, and finally give in to the temptation and squeeze her breasts.

She sobs in desire and spirals her hips on me a little faster. I grab her ass to pull her tighter against me.

She looks mind-blowing like this. She gives herself to me completely even when we're just sitting here kissing and making out. She holds nothing back.

Did she ever act like this with Landon? I can't believe that. She's all mine. She gives me something she's never given anyone else.

I don't care if it's true. I'll believe it anyway.

I bend down and nip her breasts through her top. She squeals, arches her back, and runs her fingers into my hair to pull my head into her.

She bucks against me faster when I bite her like this. She drills into me so hard she hurts me, but I don't want her to stop.

I want to take her right now, but the same feeling holds me back. I don't want to push it or rush anything. I don't need to. I want to make it last all night long.

I stand up and lower her feet to the floor. I'm not planning on doing anything except kiss her.

Her smoldering eyes float up to meet mine. She holds me in the palm of her hand when she touches the knot of my tie and starts to undo it.

Her lips quiver when she slides it out of my collar and slowly, slowly starts to unbutton my shirt. Her hands bring goosebumps out on my arms and down my legs.

I can only stand here enthralled as she works down, down, down, toward my stomach.

I speed up the process by taking off my jacket. She tugs my shirt out of my belt and unbuttons the last button. Now it's my turn. This is way easier and simpler.

I take hold of her dress. She raises her arms when I draw it over her head.

She stands in front of me in her bra and panties. She isn't as curvaceous as Zaria. Selena is slimmer, shorter, and less voluptuous, but no less beautiful.

The moon sets off every curve and all the lace of her midnight-blue bra and panties. They stand out against her pale white skin.

She presents herself in front of me in all her glory, but only for a second before she eases into me, glides her hands up my bare chest under my shirt, and wraps her arms around my waist.

Her warmth sets off a chain reaction that blows my mind apart. She hugs me close and her skin lights me on fire. Her breasts crush against my stomach and her thin body feels tiny and fragile compared to my size and weight.

I slip my fingertips into her hair and clench. She gasps in my mouth and the energy between us explodes off the charts.

I attack her mouth in ravenous bites. I can't get enough of her. I want to shove her against the wall, turn her backward, and hammer her until she screams. I never want to hear her stop screaming.

I get so worked up over her that I have to pull away. I have to slow down. I have to keep my head around her. I can't take tonight too far. I have to make sure to do it right for her.

Her expression changes in a flash. "We don't have to do this if you don't want to," she tells me. "Don't do something you aren't comfortable doing."

"No!" I husk. "I want to."

"Are you sure?" she asks. I can't believe she's the one worried about me now.

"Yes! I'm sure! I just don't want to go too fast for you."

"You won't," she tells me. "You don't have to hold back."

My head shoots up. "Are you sure?"

She nods. "I'm sure. I want this. I want to go as far as you want to go."

I gulp. Those words stab me in the guts. I want to go as far as she wants to go. There's no end to where we could go together.

I stand up straight in front of her. She wants this and I want more than anything to give her what she wants. I don't want her to leave her until she's satisfied.

I scoop my arm behind her waist, lift her off the floor, and pull her in kissing her hard and fast. I don't hold back this time.

I kiss her as deeply as I want to. I don't stop myself from showing how insatiably hungry she makes me.

She comes back at me just as hard. She straps her arms around my neck kissing me to the ends of the earth.

As soon as I lift her off the floor, she raises both legs and rests them on my hips like she wants to straddle me again. I love feeling her like this.

She doesn't stop kissing me when I carry her into the bedroom. She actually laughs out loud when I sink one knee onto the mattress and lower her onto the bed still kissing her.

I just plan to stay here on my hands and knees and kiss her for as long as it takes, but she pulls me down on top of her.

Her kiss changes, she opens her mouth all the way, coils her tongue around mine, and starts pulling my shirt off. She wraps her satin legs around my waist and clenches me in tight.

I can't hold back. I don't need to hold back. She's signaling me so clearly that she wants this. She wants me to go all the way.

My prick throbs with painful desire when I screw my hips between her legs. She moans into my mouth and then squeals again when I drive up into her hard enough to push her thighs apart.

She rocks under me, strokes her delicate hands down my back, and circles my waist until her hands come to rest on my belt buckle.

Her eyes float into focus in front of me. She holds me captive again with her sultry, intoxicating gaze when she pulls my belt loose.

That sensation shoots straight to my crotch. She's actually doing this. She's about to take my pants off.

I don't know if I'll be able to hold myself back if she does that, but I can't stop her. I know that now. Anything she wants to do to me, I'll just have to lie here and take it.

I want her to. I want her to touch me any way she wants. I want her to feel like she owns me.

I want to touch her back. I want to devour every succulent inch of her, but I have to hold myself up on my arms to give her space to work.

My belt falls open, but she doesn't stop there. She unbuttons my pants. I stare at her in abject shock when she slides my zipper down, slithers her small hand into my shorts, and takes hold of me.

I groan through bared teeth when she starts to stroke me. "Look at me, Reese," she whispers. "Look at me."

I fight to maintain eye contact, but I'm growling, wincing, and howling too much. Her hand feels unbelievable. I have no choice but to pump into her hand building up to something I'm not sure I can survive.

Her sex-drunk eyes hover in front of me. They hold me as tightly as her hand. She clamps down when she feels me strain against her fingers. She doesn't let up—and then she burrows her other hand down there and takes hold of my balls.

I can't stand this. I try to dive in and kiss her, but I wind up exploding in her hands instead. I bellow in an agony of release. I can't remember ever climaxing like this—with anyone.

I rest my forehead on her shoulder roaring and practically sobbing as the dam breaks. She can't be doing me like this. She can't be giving me this when I want to be the one to send her to the stars.

She kisses the side of my head. "You're so beautiful," she whispers into my brain.

How can she say that about me when she is so mind-blowingly beautiful? How can she see me that way when we barely know each other?

I don't even get a chance to stop moaning before she pulls her hands out, scoots down underneath me, and pulls my shorts down enough to take me in her mouth.

I'm so sensitive from what she just did that I wind up wincing again. Her mouth drives me insane.

My body reacts and thrusts all the way into her mouth again and again. She makes me so damn hard all over again. I could cum in her mouth right now, but I don't want to. I want to give her just a little of the pleasure she's giving me.

I find it nearly impossible not to drill her head down onto the mattress. I could seriously plow into her mouth right now.

I summon all my effort to tear myself away from her. I have to keep my head even though she's already completely blown my mind.

She studies me in uncertain confusion when I rear off her. She lies under me sprawled on the bed in her bra and panties. Does she really think I would let her take care of me like that without reciprocating?

I kiss her chest, breasts, and stomach while I work my way down to her panties. She whimpers when I slide them off and sink between her thighs. Tonight is going to be a long night. I might as well start with the appetizer.

Chapter 9: Selena

I writhe over onto my side still seething in torment from all the orgasms Reese keeps giving me. He's been lying down there between my legs fingering and licking me for I don't know how long.

I don't know if I can handle how having sex with him makes me feel. It brings us closer together. It bonds us in ways nothing else can.

I sure wish I knew where this was going.

I don't have to wonder when he crawls up the bed, unclips my bra while I'm lying on my side, and then rolls me toward him.

He isn't wearing his pants anymore. He must have pushed them off while he was eating me out.

He pulls my bra off and lowers himself between my legs the way he did before—except that we're both naked now.

He glides into me so effortlessly that I can only sigh in relief. His mouth and fingers have prepared me so thoroughly to take him.

His body contracts when he thrusts in all the way to my limit. I spiral into another dizzy orgasm. "Look at me, baby," he whispers.

My eyes drift open. The tempest of blissful emotion and rushing pleasure sweep through me. I look into his deepest soul and they skyrocket me off the charts.

I see his heart written there. I see the man who has been so kind and attentive to me since this started.

He's the man who shares my darkest secrets—the man who fulfills my hidden desires—and not just the sexual ones.

His stiff shaft splits me apart with every brutal thrust. My heart breaks open for him.

He adjusts his position, scoops up one of my legs, and bends my knee all the way back to my shoulder to stretch me wide.

He sees me whine and sob for him to take me all the way. He sees me completely exposed and vulnerable to whatever he wants to do to me.

Before I know what he's doing, he pivots my knee across my body and pushes me over onto my side. He keeps my leg up, and before I know what's happening, he starts slamming into me from behind.

He bends in low and husks in my ear as I flounder to steady myself on my arms. "Take it," he rasps. "Take it nice and hard."

I scream as those wicked words blast me into another reeling climax. I can't stop as long as he keeps taking me.

"You want it bad, don't you?" he snarls. "You want to take it hard and dirty like that."

"Yes!!" I shriek.

"You want to be my wicked little pleasure, don't you? You want to spread it wide open and take me all the way. Come on. Come on. Give it to me like you know you want to."

I can't stop screaming. He knows exactly what I need, and in an instant, he wraps his arm around my shoulders from behind and pulls me up onto my knees.

I can't hold myself up like this, but he holds onto me tighter than tight.

He crushes me against his iron body while he spikes into me from behind. His power builds to the breaking point. I can't take this. I can only scream and scream and scream from the colossal intensity of what he's doing to me.

I see myself as dirty, trashy, and animalistic. I'm as filthy and slutty as Zaria—but this is somehow cleaner and almost sacred.

My body belongs to him in ways I've never belonged to anyone before. I give more of myself and don't guard myself against anything, not even this.

Without thinking first, I slide my hand behind me and grab his balls. I don't know why. I just want to. I like to touch him. I like giving him pleasure and feeling his body while he gives me pleasure.

He roars in my ear, slams in hard at my touch, and his powerful load floods me with his essence. His shaft spasms and his balls shrink as they contract upward into him.

I massage them in my hand, try to relax them, and tug them down. He groans and howls every time I do it.

I love the way he sounds when he cums. I love the way his features tense and twist. I love making him howl and moan like that because he feels so good.

We both collapse onto the bed, but I don't let go of him. He curls in behind me still gasping and growling as I fondle him.

He wraps his arms and body around me from behind, but I want to see him. I squirm over onto my other side so I can face him. I don't stop playing with him.

He keeps his eyes shut until I push him onto his back. I worship his body. He stretches out like a god, turns his head away, and winces again when I play with his balls.

"God damn, baby," he whispers. "That feels so damn good."

I love it when he says things like that. Landon never told me anything I did felt good.

I want to do more, but Reese is already going soft.

I sink down on him and take his balls in my mouth. I want to suck him properly, but I can do that later.

He convulses when I suck one of his balls into my mouth. He gasps and his hand flies to my head. "Oh, my God, baby! Don't stop! Holy shit!" he husks.

I wrap my tongue around his sack. He's already starting to get hard again.

I suck his other ball for a minute, but his shaft proves too strong a temptation. I take him and stroke down on him. He won't stop groaning, growling, and running his fingers through my hair as I pick up speed.

I want to make him cum again, but he stops me. He pulls me off, takes hold of my arms, and guides me up him to straddle his rigid shaft.

I sink down on it, but he won't let me kiss him. He holds onto both of my arms so I sit up straight in front of him.

I can't hold back my moans when I look down at him. It's already three o'clock in the morning. We've been doing it for hours with no sign of stopping. I don't want to stop. I want to keep going—maybe forever.

He bucks his hips into me from below and makes me whimper when I feel another epic climax building up in me. Will it ever end?

"You're an angel," he whispers.

I rest my hands on his chest. "You're a hero," I whisper back.

He bursts out in a huge, blushing grin. "You're a sex goddess."

I find myself laughing along with him. "You're a porn star."

He explodes in laughter. "Don't tell Zaria that."

"Would she be jealous if she saw the way we're doing it?"

"Oh, hell yes! She would never let you near me again."

I can't stop smiling and blushing at him even as he drives me to another bone-crushing crescendo.

"You're mine," I whisper.

He gets serious instantly. "I'm yours. Do whatever you want with me."

I can't help but grin again. "I already am."

"Good." He bumps his hips up into me. "I want to see you cum for me again."

I moan as a delirious surge of power hits me in the head. I'm about to cum for him again.

"Would Landon be jealous if he saw the way we're doing it?" he asks.

I float back to reality enough to answer. "I'm pretty sure he already is jealous just from seeing the way I look at you."

Now it's his turn to blush. "You're all mine."

I collapse on top of him and my hair falls over him when I kiss him. "I'm all yours. Do whatever you want with me."

He grabs me around the waist, lifts me up, and slams into me from below. He has to yell over my screams to make himself heard. "I already am!"

I scream again and again, but he stops in a minute and pushes me upright.

"I'm never going to stop," he tells me when I spiral my hips on top of him. "You're going to need a wheelchair to go back to him."

"I'm never going to stop," I whisper. "You won't be able to get it up when you go back to Zaria."

He laughs and turns bright red. "That would definitely make her jealous."

My smile fades as the reality of what I'm saying sinks in. "Don't let me go back." My voice cracks with emotion. "I don't want to go back."

He pulls me down on top of me and kisses me endlessly before he eases off enough to answer.

"If you stay on me like this, you'll be too out of your mind with sex to go back. You won't even remember that you're supposed to go back."

I kiss him again. He doesn't grab me and slam into me. He doesn't push me upright again, either.

Straddling him like this ignites my desire. I buck and kick against him as the avalanche buries me under a landslide of pleasure, fulfillment, and deep emotion.

Chapter 10: Selena

I squint and immediately bury my head under the pillow when sunshine stabs me in the eyes. I groan and roll over.

Then I smell an unfamiliar smell. It smells like a man, but it isn't Landon.

My eyes pop open when I remember last night with Reese—except that it wasn't just last night. The sky was already starting to get light the last time we did it before we both passed out.

He sprawls on his stomach in front of me with both arms stretched out to the sides. He lies with his face toward me. He's sound asleep.

I collapse back in bed. I'm surrounded by soft, clean white sheets with a dozen pillows under my head. I've never been more comfortable.

My body feels rubbery and slack from all that sex. I'm also sore and exhausted, but I've never felt more content with myself.

He really is some kind of god in bed. He can go forever and he always makes me orgasm. I don't even know how many orgasms I had last night—and this morning.

I start to drift off when he stirs. He groans, squints at the sunshine streaming through the windows, and rolls over before he pulls a pillow over his face. "Wake me up when it's nighttime again," he grumbles. "I've decided to become a vampire."

"You and me both." I curl up behind him, wrap my arms around him, and shut my eyes.

I really do drift off and wake up a few hours later. I don't even know what time it is, but I should probably get back to Landon.

I crane my head off the pillows enough to see the clock. It's eleven in the morning.

I collapse on the bed groaning again, but I groan more from exasperation that I have to go back to him at all. I'm sure he'll be in a state of high anxiety that I've been gone for so long.

I roll onto my back trying to work up the energy to get out of bed. I stare at the ceiling and run my fingers through my hair while I decide what I'm going to say to him.

The truth will probably be best. Better for him to hear the hard truth than to soften the blow with a lie. Maybe then he'll get it through his thick head that it really is over.

If his cheating wasn't enough to destroy our marriage, last night definitely ended it. If I can feel this with a guy like Reese, I have no reason to waste my time with Landon.

He never gave me a night like that, not even in the early days. He had all that wild sex with who knows how many women, but it didn't improve his performance in bed with me.

I might have been willing to overlook his transgressions if it did. Keyword: might have.

Reese lifts his head, takes one look at the clock, and lets out a matching groan. I laugh at him when he pulls the pillow back over his head.

"I'm officially on vacation from reality," he tells me from under the pillow.

I slip my arms around his waist from behind again. "What are you going to tell her?"

"I'm going to tell her that you gave me the best night of non-stop sex that I've ever had in my life," he mumbles. "I'm going to tell her that she needs to start taking lessons from you—which is the truth."

I kiss his back and shoulders. "I'm going to tell Landon the same thing."

Reese flips onto his back and stares up at me. "Really? You mean it?"

"Of course. Do you think I do it with guys like this all the time?" I bend in and kiss him.

I want to kiss him long and deep, but he pushes me back. "You're serious. You really mean it."

"Yes, Reese," I tell him. "You mean it about me, don't you?"

"Of course. Do you think I do it with girls like this all the time?"

I want to laugh, but I only wilt in disappointment instead. "I guess we have to go back. It's already late."

He rears off the bed and props himself on his elbow. "Don't leave! Stay. Stay here." He kisses me. "We'll order room service. We don't have to leave."

My eyes fall out of their sockets. "Are you serious? You mean like...don't go back?"

"I mean stay....for the day.....and however long. Don't leave just yet. This is too good."

He kisses me again and this isn't just a quick kiss on the lips. He stays there, and before either of us can even think, we're kissing as never before—except that we have done it all before. We've done it a lot of times before and we'll do it a lot of times again.

He uses his mouth to push me back down onto the bed. He climbs on top of me and then has to pull the sheet out of the way so he can work his way inside me.

I scream again as the energy takes off. Nothing changes no matter how many times we do it.

He won't stop kissing me as his shoulders strain to hold him up. His hair falls over his eyes. I can't look at him as I burst into another delirious climax. He snarls at me and then roars out as the wave breaks.

I could keep going, but he rolls off and sits up on the edge of the bed. "What do you want to order for room service?" he asks over his shoulder.

"You," I tell him and make him laugh.

"Then I'll have you." He rolls over and burrows his face between my legs.

"Hey!" I try to grab him, but he's already exciting me. "Hey—you're gonna wind up tasting yourself if you do that."

"It tastes like us." He grunts a few times. "This is so much more satisfying than food."

I buck my hips into his face as his fingers split me apart. He keeps me dangling on the edge of bliss until I dissolve in another mind-blowing orgasm.

I collapse in a sodden heap of whimpering sobs trying to hold myself together. He crawls up my body kissing me everywhere. He tries to kiss me on the mouth, but I'm too out of my mind to think straight.

He topples onto his back and pulls me into his arms. He holds me while he picks up the room service menu.

He doesn't ask me what I want. He's still holding me when he puts the menu on the mattress next to him, wakes up his phone, and makes the call.

He orders a whole bunch of dishes, snacks, desserts, and non-alcoholic drinks.

"Aren't you going to call Zaria?" I ask after he hangs up.

"Hell no," he snaps. "And you aren't going to call Landon. We'll stay holed up in here for the rest of the damn cruise. They'll have to call the authorities before they find us."

I find myself laughing. "We could survive in here for the rest of the cruise with all that food you ordered."

"We won't eat it all. We'll be too busy nailing each other."

I laugh again and fall back on the pillows to look up at him. "You're really enjoying this, aren't you?"

"Of course. Can't you tell by my bubbly, vivacious personality?"

I blush and giggle. "Yeah, that kinda gave it away."

He flips over on his side, rests his head on the pillow, and curls up to gaze at me. "Do you want to talk some more?"

"What do you want to talk about?"

"Everything," he replies. "I could talk to you all day and night. We don't have to have sex."

"Um.....okay. Do you have any hobbies?"

"Motorcycles used to be my hobby, but now it's my job."

"Do you have any hobbies now?"

He looks away. "You'll say it's stupid."

"No, I won't! You said you want to know everything about me. I want to know everything about you."

He turns away. "I might as well pack up my stuff now...."

"Reese! Don't you dare! Now you have to tell me!"

"Okay, fine." He falls down on the pillow and grins at me. "I like scuba diving."

My jaw drops. "No way."

He grins. "Yeah. I save up my money and go on month-long vacations in equatorial countries where I can scuba dive and see all kinds of underwater life. Last year I went to the Great Barrier Reef. I want to go back, but I decided to go to the Florida Keys next year."

I can't stop staring at him. "You're joking, right? You aren't pulling my leg?"

His smile fades. "That bad, huh? I knew you wouldn't like it."

"I like scuba diving, Reese! It's one of my favorite things to do!"

The color drains from his cheeks. "Really?"

"YES!! I got certified when I was in college. I used to go all the time, but I stopped when I married Landon because he wasn't interested. I can't believe this!" I grab him. "We have to go! The ship is making a few stops where we can go diving. We have to! We're going to do this together."

He blinks at me. "Really? You aren't just saying that?"

"No way! This is gonna be great. When are you going to Florida? I want to go."

"You do? For real?"

I laugh at his reaction. "Did you really think I wouldn't like it?"

"Do you like motorcycles?"

I blush at him. "I like riding on the back. I've never ridden one by myself before."

"I can work with that." He lies down. "What else do you like?"

"I like using my art and making beautiful homemade notebooks."

"Nope," he counters. "Not interesting at all."

I laugh at him. "What else do you like?"

"I like birdwatching."

"Yeah!" I exclaim. "I love that. I love drawing them into my homemade notebooks."

He makes a face. "I'm a photography guy."

"I can work with that."

He splits into a grin. "This is gonna be great."

"Yeah!" I giggle again, but right then, someone knocks on the door. The room service guy calls from out in the corridor.

Reese tells him to hold on a second, puts on his pants, and I hide under the covers while the guy wheels his cart in. Reese tips him.

"You can come out now," Reese tells me after he shuts the door.

I sit up and he pulls the cart over to the bed so we can tear into the food.

Chapter 11: Reese

I lie on the bed with my arm around Selena while we watch the sun go down outside our suite balcony. We haven't left this room in twenty-four hours.

I feel completely drained physically, mentally, and emotionally after spending all this amazing time with her—and it isn't just the sex.

This is hands down the most emotional sex I've ever had. She connects with me at an emotional level when we do it.

I feel myself starting to fall for her. I don't want to lose this.

I don't ever want to do it with anyone else again. I want to keep her with me always so we can keep feeling this way about each other.

The blazing golden sun touches the black surface of the ocean out there on the horizon. The orange-yellow streak of light melts into the rim of the Earth.

"I guess we have to go soon," she murmurs.

I press my lips against her head and stroke my fingers through her hair. "Don't go back to him. Stay here with me for the rest of the cruise."

She turns her face downward and kisses my chest. "Do you mean it?"

"Yes," I breathe. "I can rent this suite for the rest of the cruise. Your suite and mine are already paid for. Landon and Zaria can stay there.

I don't want this to end and I definitely don't want you to go back to him. Stay here with me. Let's keep it going for as long as it lasts."

She leans back to look up at me. "You're serious. You really mean it."

"Absolutely. Don't tell me you want to go."

"Of course I don't. This is perfect the way it is."

"Then why change it? It feels right. Let's keep doing it. We've both already broken up with them. We don't have to explain anything to anyone. This is too good. Come on. Stay with me."

She sighs and tips over to cuddle into me again. "All right. I don't want to leave anyway. I suppose I should go back sometime to get my stuff out of the suite. I'll need to take a shower and brush my teeth and some point."

I laugh. "If you absolutely have to….brush your teeth, I mean."

She joins in the joke. "You wouldn't like me very much if I didn't. You would beg me to go back to Landon."

"He could have you if you didn't brush your teeth."

I kiss her on the hair. I can think of so many things I want to do with her, but I'm too tired right now. I haven't slept in two days and neither has she. We both need rest.

I scoot down further into bed and pull her toward me, but we can't see the sunset like this.

She rolls onto her other side, spoons back into me, and I turn over so we can both look out past the balcony.

"How did this get to be so good?" she murmurs.

I kiss the back of her head. "I guess it was just meant to be."

She sighs. She feels it, too. Her voice gets farther away as she drifts off. "We'll need to order breakfast in the morning."

I murmur something under my breath as my eyes sink closed. Holding her is one of the best feelings I've ever felt.

I completely forget about everything else until I wake up in the morning. The sun is just coming up and Selena lies tucked into my arms the way she fell asleep last night.

I bend my head down and she mews in her sleep when I kiss her neck. She feels delicious.

I try to lie still, but holding her like this makes me start to get hard for her. I don't mean to wake her up, but before I think to stop her, she moves her hand behind her and takes hold of my rigid shaft.

I clench my teeth in a brutal groan when she starts stroking me. Her hand makes me ache to be inside her, but I can't do that when she touches me like this.

She squirms her other hand behind her and grabs my balls in such a gentle hold. She knows exactly how to handle me to make me crumble for her.

I feel myself starting to escalate too fast. Is she going to finish me off like this? I don't know if I can handle that.

I'm just about to attack her when she lets go, turns over, and weasels down in the bed. She inhales me into her mouth before I think to stop her.

Her mouth seizes me in a death grip and she sucks the life out of me. I can't hold back. My head rolls back and I explode into her mouth roaring and howling in an agony of pleasure.

She sucks every drop from me and even swirls her tongue around my nuts before she kisses my prick once and leans back. "Is that breakfast taken care of for me?"

I groan again when I roll onto my back. "It better not be."

She fumbles over me and grabs my phone off the bedside table. "Let's order. I'm still hungry."

I snort. "You're a demon, aren't you?"

"I have a big appetite."

"You aren't big enough to have a big appetite. Give me that."

I take the phone and the menu away from her. She grins at me and goes to the bathroom while I place the order. She comes back all naked in a minute.

"I should go get my stuff out of Landon's suite," she tells me. "I guess you should do the same thing."

"Fine, but come here first." I stretch out on my back and brush my hands across my cheeks. "I'm making a nice place for you to sit."

She stares at me. "Are you crazy?"

"Come up here and sit on my face. That's an order."

She doesn't move.

"What's wrong? Don't you want to? We don't have to."

"But....won't I hurt you?"

"Of course not. Are you telling me you've never sat on a guy's face before?"

"No, never. Are you sure it's safe?"

I laugh at her. "It's time to lose your virginity, sweetheart. Come up here and ride my face exactly the same way you would be riding my prick if you were on top. Come on. You only live once. I promise you won't hurt me."

"Have you done this before?"

"Not nearly enough times. Come on. I want you."

She takes a few steps toward me. "I don't know about this....."

"I do. Come on. You had me. Now I'm going to have you. You better hurry up or the room service boy will hear you."

She colors and climbs onto the bed. I relax onto my back as she positions her thighs on either side of my head.

I stroke her up to her hips and pull her down onto my mouth. Mmm. She's delectable.

She moans when she starts riding my face. I lick her as fast as I can, but she loses control soon enough.

She rides down hard, suffocates me, and starts bucking as she screams. She grabs the headboard and uses it as leverage to drill down on my face.

I jam my fingers into her and her sweet honey gushes into my mouth. She screams again and again riding me to kingdom come before she falls off moaning on the bed.

I'm just sitting up to pull her onto her knees from behind when the room service guy knocks on the door.

I throw the sheets over her and pull on my pants before I meet him. I tip him, take the cart, and shut the door.

"Come eat some real food, baby," I tell her. "You need fuel for when you go give Landon his daily spanking."

She groans and rolls over onto her other side. She rakes her fingers through her hair before she looks up at me, but she still looks all melted and fragile from that.

"Is there anything else I should know about?" she asks. "Any other sexual activities you plan to introduce me to?"

I grin at her. "We can save that for the second date."

She snorts and crawls over to me to share the breakfast.

I try not to watch her too closely. Her body drives me crazy. She's so incredibly sweet and receptive. I can't wait to spend the rest of the cruise in this room with her—except that I don't plan to spend the rest of the cruise in this room with her.

I'll take her out. I'll wine her and dine her and show her off. We'll have the time of our lives together. I want to go scuba diving with her and birdwatching and everything. I can just picture all the possibilities.

She finally takes a shower and puts on the dress she wore that first night. I put on my suit.

She carries her heels in her hand. She looks much more casual like this.

She makes a face when she looks down at herself. "I hope Landon doesn't get any ideas when he sees me like this."

I pull out my phone. "Give me your number. You can call me if he gives you a hard time. I'll come and get you."

She beams at me and gives me the number. "Thank you. I really appreciate it. I wish I could help you out with Zaria, but I think you might be on your own with that one."

"I'll handle her. Don't let Landon give you any static. You can do so much better."

She colors again and kisses me on the cheek. "I am. I'll see you in a little while."

She slips out of the room. I ride the elevator downstairs and go to the purser's office. I rent that suite for the rest of the cruise and make sure to take my name off the other one. That way, I won't have to pay for it if Zaria trashes it.

I go back upstairs and return to the suite I used to share with Zaria. She isn't there. I go into the other room and start packing my suitcase. I've never been happier to get the hell out of anywhere.

She comes back when I'm in the middle of the job. "Where have you been?!" she demands. "You've been gone for three days!"

"I told you. I've been with Selena."

Her jaw drops. "You've been with her all this time?!"

I nod and wind up smirking when I see her reaction. I don't even care if I hurt her feelings. "Yeah. She's great."

"You....." Her eyes narrow when she sees that smirk. "What have you been doing?"

I make a face. "You don't want to know—or maybe you do. I'm sure you can use your imagination and it still wouldn't even come close. You really need to start taking lessons from her."

She glares at me and then gasps when she sees me zipping my suitcase closed. "What are you doing?"

"I'm moving out of this suite. Selena is splitting up with her husband. We're moving into the suite I rented for the last two nights. We're going to spend the rest of the cruise together."

"You can't do that! The couples swap was only supposed to be for one hookup—not the whole cruise! Reese!! What are you doing?"

Her voice spikes off the charts when I put the suitcase on its wheels on the floor. I push it out of the room and head for the door to leave the suite.

She grabs my arm to hold me back. "STOP!!" she shrieks. "You can't do this to me!!"

I turn around extra slowly. I'm so far gone with this woman that I can't even get mad at her anymore.

"Answer me one question," I tell her. "If you tell the truth just this once, I might consider giving you another chance. I'm not making any promises. Just tell the truth. I'll know if you're lying. This is your only chance."

"Anything!" she exclaims. "I'll do anything! You can't leave me, Reese! I love you! I never did anything with Landon. I swear it! I only want to be with you!"

I raise my index finger to silence her. "Answer me one question."

"Anything!" she pants again.

"How many guys did you sleep with while we were together—and I mean all of them—the real number? Don't you dare lie about it."

She opens her mouth to say—and stops herself. She stares at me for a second before she shuts her mouth.

I nod, grab my suitcase handle, and turn back to the door. "That's the only answer I need."

"No, Reese!" she shrieks. "I love you!"

I don't answer. I don't turn around. I'm totally, completely, in every way done with her.

I pull away from her and push my suitcase out of the room. She follows me into the corridor practically screaming about how much she loves me. She has a funny way of showing it.

I stop in the corridor, turn around, take hold of her arm, and shove her back inside the room before I shut the door in her face.

I hear her break down crying in there behind the door, but I don't care. She's broken my heart a dozen times. She won't do it again, now that I finally found someone I care about.

Chapter 12: Selena

I walk into the suite and almost collide with Landon. He's pacing around the living room running his fingers through his hair.

He spins around to confront me the minute I walk in. "Where have you been?!" he gasps. "I've been worried sick about you!"

"You didn't need to be." I walk away toward my room. "I've been with Reese having the time of my life."

"Reese!" he counters. "That was three days ago!"

"I've been with him in the suite all this time. We never set foot out of the door until just now." I give into the temptation to smirk at him. "He's great. He really knows what he's doing in the bedroom, I can tell you."

I get a cruel thrill when he flinches. "You...you've been in bed with him for three days?"

"Yeah! I can barely walk this morning." I throw my suitcase on the bed and start going back and forth between the closet, the dresser, and the suitcase to pack up my things. "He's introducing me to things I've never tried before. It's fantastic. I really have to thank you. You were right. This is going to be the best thing for me."

"You can't see him again! The couples swap was only supposed to be one time."

"Nice try, but no," I reply over my shoulder. "I'm moving out so I can spend the rest of the cruise with him."

He gapes at me in horror. "You can't do that! That wasn't part of the deal!"

"The only deal was that you betrayed me and I dumped you. We aren't married anymore so I can do what I want. So are you. You can go enjoy yourself. Have fun. Maybe you'll meet someone who introduces you to things you've never tried before."

He strides into the room and stands there jabbering at me while I pack. "You can't do this, Selena! We're still married!"

"Only on paper."

"I love you! I never did anything with Zaria! I swear it. She was all ready to go, but I couldn't because I couldn't stop thinking about you."

I snort in his face. "You couldn't stop thinking about me with Reese, you mean. You didn't care about porking everything that walks as long as you knew I was sitting at home waiting for you. All of this was your idea, Landon, so you have no one to blame but yourself."

"Hey! You can't move out! We're supposed to be working this out."

"We are working it out. We're working it out by splitting up. I only regret that I didn't do it a long time ago—but then I wouldn't have met Reese. I really owe you for that one. Thank you."

He stands there in stunned horror while I finish packing my stuff. I really don't care if this hurts his feelings. In fact, I hope it does.

I hope he spends the rest of his life flinching in agony when he thinks about Reese doing it with me for three days straight.

We didn't. We ate. We slept. We cuddled. We talked.

Landon doesn't need to know that. He doesn't need to know how much I love making Reese cum. Landon doesn't need to know that Reese and I share a love of scuba diving and birdwatching.

I just don't care about Landon anymore. I really just don't care if he sleeps with other women. I hope he does. I hope he meets someone who can give him some small part of what Reese gives me.

Landon is still standing there in shocked silence when I wheel my suitcase out of the room. I expect him to make more of a scene, but he doesn't. He just stands there looking defeated. Finally.

I wheel my suitcase back down the corridor to the suite I'm going to be sharing with Reese. He isn't there. I can't get in without the key.

I stand there wondering what I should do when he shows up in his suit. He waves the key at me. "Looking for this?"

I grin. "Yeah. I was just wondering if I made a terrible mistake."

He hands it to me. "This is yours." He uses his key to open the suite.

His suitcase is already inside. I heft mine onto the bed and unzip it. "How did it go with you-know-who?"

"You mean Voldemort?" he asks and makes me laugh. "She was distraught. She swears up and down she didn't do it with Landon....."

I spin around. "Did she say why?"

"No, she just said she loves me and I can't do this to her and she swears she never did it with him."

I snort at him. "That's because he got cold feet. He says she was ready to roll, but he couldn't stop thinking about me being with you. I'm pretty sure hearing about us scarred him for life."

"Dang. Poor guy."

"Oh, don't start saying 'poor guy' in relation to Landon! He's a sleaze. He got what he deserved."

He sits down in the armchair across the room. "Yeah. I get that now. Zaria got what she deserved, too."

"Maybe they'll get together with each other. I'm quite sure she can teach him to lie down while she sits on his face."

He chuckles. "I'm sure she can. I told her I would give her another chance if she told me the truth about how many guys she did it with while we were together."

I spin around to stare at him. "What did she say?"

"She refused to answer—so that tells you something."

I shake my head while I fold the rest of my things into the dresser. "Wow. It must have been a lot."

"I can only imagine. Do you have any other nice dresses besides that one?"

"I have a few. Why?"

"I want to take you out to dinner tonight."

I stare at him. "You do?"

"Yes. I want us to have dinner and maybe see a show. I want to enjoy this cruise with you and do it right."

I burst out in a big blushing smile. "I would love that."

"Do whatever you have to do to get ready. I can wait."

"It's still morning. Don't you want to do anything?"

"Anything like what? Do you mean anything other than rolling around in bed with you?"

I try to look away to stop him from seeing my cheeks color. "Yes. I mean anything other than rolling around in bed with me."

"We could go around the ship and see what there is to see and do.....but maybe we should wait until Landon and Zaria have a few minutes to readjust to the new reality."

I smile over my shoulder at him. "Maybe you should unpack first—and maybe change into something more casual."

"Oh, right. I completely forgot."

We spend the next hour and a half taking showers, changing our clothes into something more casual, and putting the rest of our clothes and belongings away to spend the rest of the cruise in this suite.

We wind up talking about all kinds of stuff after that—philosophy, politics, pets, family, our childhoods—you name it.

It's already getting late in the afternoon by the time we finish. Now it's time to start getting ready to go out.

Reese finishes getting dressed first and sits down at the living room table to check the ship's program. "There are a few interesting shows on tonight. We could go to one of them after dinner."

I shoot him a smirk. "Are you sure you can stand to stay out of the bedroom that long?"

He laughs and now he's the one who blushes. "We'll see who can go the longest without dragging the other one back here by the hair for sexual conquest."

I gasp in mock horror. "Since when have I ever conquered you sexually? I'm offended."

He makes a face. "Please. You were the one who did it to me first that night. Don't act all innocent now."

"I thought you liked it."

"I did. I loved it—and I still do. I'm just saying don't play all innocent and coy and make it out like I'm the only one who does the conquering in this relationship. We both know I'm not."

I sidle over to him in my bra and panties, slip my arms around his neck, and kiss him. "Are we in a relationship?"

"We're living together in this suite and going out to dinner and a show. I think we're in a relationship—but we won't be going anywhere if you don't get dressed."

He gives me a playful smack on the ass and makes me yelp. "Ooo!" I tease. "What a beast you are!"

He grabs me, spins me around, tips me over his knee, and spanks me five more times hard enough to make me scream.

"You know what happens to bad girls!" he snaps behind me. "You better behave yourself or suffer the consequences."

I scream again as he delivers the last smack. Then he pushes me upright to stand on my own feet.

I turn around to face him. Him spanking me makes me ache for so much more. My flesh throbs and quivers between my legs. I give him my smokiest, sexiest look and glide closer to him.

"Are you trying to turn me on?" I ask.

"Did it turn you on to get spanked?"

I ease a little closer, straddle his leg, and ride it while I moan in deep, hungry need. "I need you so bad!" I whine. "Oh, please! Oh, please!"

I'm getting so turned on I could orgasm right now.

He seizes me by the ass, crushes me into his leg a few times, and pushes me away. "If you behave I might take care of you later. Now go get dressed and don't let me see you act like that in public."

I take a step back, laugh, and narrow my eyes at him. "Oooo! It is such a turn-on when you act all authoritative like that! You can conquer me anytime you want to."

He smirks and turns back to the program. "Don't tempt me."

"That's what I'm trying to do."

He doesn't take the bait, so I guess I have no choice but to go get dressed like he told me to.

This relationship is turning into something so much more than I thought it would be. Where will it end?

Chapter 13: Reese

I have to summon all my self-control not to fool around with Selena on our way down to the main concourse. She looks absolutely jaw-dropping in another tight white dress with a large bow right there at the corner of her hip.

I can't look at her curves without spiraling off into fantasies about all the wicked things I want to do to her.

She really knows how to tease me with her sexy ways. I probably would have stayed in the suite with her, bent her over, spanked her until she screamed, and then did a bunch of other things to make her scream.

We do need to go out sometimes. I don't want our relationship to be only about the bedroom.

She catches me eyeing her on our way down the elevator. I could put my arm around her and grope her in the elevator. No one else is here to see us.

I satisfy myself by just holding her hand. I'll take her when we go back to the suite. There will always be enough time for that.

I want to spend tonight talking to her. Talking to her thrills me almost as much as the sex. Sometimes I think talking to her thrills me more than the sex.

It's scary how much we have in common. The connection when we talk is like nothing I've ever experienced with anyone, not even my family and closest friends.

I'm really looking forward to it when I lead her into a restaurant on the concourse. This isn't the exclusive, expensive restaurant upstairs. This one is bigger and busier, but it has a homey, comfortable atmosphere even though it has more patrons.

"So what kind of shows interest you?" I ask when we sit down at the table. "Do you like musicals?"

"They aren't my favorite."

"Oh, good, because they aren't my favorite, either."

"Do you have something specific picked out?" she asks. "Just tell me if you do. We have enough time. We can see a lot of different things."

"I don't have anything specific picked out. I was hoping we could narrow it down to a few key genres. We could see some musical acts, theater productions, comedy……"

"I would be happy to see any of those."

"Mongrel Pack is on at the Hutchinson Comedy Club," I tell her. "That looks like a good act."

She cocks her head to frown at me. "I've never heard of it."

"It's a two-man act. I've seen clips from them. They're pretty funny."

"Great! Let's do it."

"That was way easier than I thought it would be."

She laughs. "Don't read too much into it. We still have the rest of the cruise to get into our first fight."

"Or we could become one of those couples that never fights. We could just settle our disagreements and miscommunications like rational adults."

"Yeah! Let's do that."

I find myself laughing with her. The waiter comes to take our order and leaves.

"So what are we talking about tonight?" I ask.

"What haven't we covered?"

"What are your career goals?" I ask.

"I might like to do an animated film," she tells me.

My eyebrows fly up. "You would? That sounds incredible."

"It would be if I could stop procrastinating and actually do it. It would require a commitment of a lot of my free time over the course of probably years. I'm not sure I'm ready for that."

"Hmm. That does sound intimidating. I can see why you hesitate to do it."

"What about you?" she asks. "What are your career goals? I'm sure you don't want to be a salesman forever."

"I love being a salesman, but what I love about it is talking to people. I want to start a website that would be kind of a combination blog, podcast, forum, community, and education network all in one."

Her eyes fall open. "Seriously? That sounds incredible. What do you have to do to make something like that happen?"

"Well, I already have the website, blog, podcast, and forum. It's still small now because it's so new, but it's growing. I'm working on monetizing it by creating courses, selling e-books, and offering consulting services to people doing restorations or who want to get into the industry."

She gasps and her jaw drops. "You're doing all of that?! No way!"

I nod and bite back a grin at her reaction. "Yeah. It takes a lot of work, but it's worth it."

"I can't believe this!" she exclaims. "I'm amazed! How are you doing all of that?"

I shrug. "I just do a little at a time here and there when I have time."

She shuts her mouth and gulps. "That's incredible."

I laugh nervously. "Zaria didn't approve. She thought it was a huge waste of time."

All the color drains from her cheeks. "You're kidding."

"Nope. She told me a million times to give it up."

"Wow." Selena turns away. "I'm stunned that you stayed with her this long."

"She thinks it's a hobby or a pastime. She thinks it's a distraction from what really matters in life."

She shakes her head. "I don't think that. I think it's amazing that you're doing all of that. I can't wait to see it all."

I frown. "What do you mean?"

"I want to see it. I want to read your content and hear your podcasts and see the website. I want to see what you're doing and all the courses you're selling."

"But you aren't interested in motorcycles—not in that way. You aren't into restoration or repair or anything like that."

"I'm interested in you. I want to see what you're interested in and I want to get involved if I can." Now she's the one who frowns. "I don't know how an illustrator could help you with it, but I will if I can. Anyway, I want to support you. I think it's so admirable that you're following your passion. It's inspiring for me to get started on my own project."

I can't answer. I just sit in silence and stare at her. We're barely dating and she's already saying she wants to support my ambitions.

If I ever questioned her, all of that doubt goes out the window. She's the one.

She's right about Zaria. I should have dumped her the very instant she said a bad word about my website project. I should have taken it as a sign from On High to get as far the hell away from her as possible.

The waiter comes back with our food and drinks. Selena and I settle down to eat our meal, but she won't stop talking about my project. She's a thousand times more interested in that than doing her own animated film.

I need to support her in that. I need to encourage her to start it. She needs her own project. She can't put all her energy into mine. She needs something she can call her own.

I put the first bite of my food into my mouth when she murmurs under her breath. "Oh, no! Brace yourself."

I look up at her. "Huh? What's wrong?"

Her eyes swivel to the other side of the restaurant. I follow her gaze and my heart stops when I see Landon coming toward us.

The other nearby patrons don't notice anything unusual until he stops in front of our table. I decide to meet the assault head on. "Can I help you with something, man?" I ask.

He glares at me and then Selena. "You have no right to swoop in and steal another man's wife. That isn't what we agreed."

"You're the one who has no right to be here, Landon," Selena interjects. "I told you it was over between us long before anything happened between me and Reese."

"We agreed it would only be the one time," Landon fires back.

"We never said that at all," I tell him. "You never said that once when we were talking about it. You said you would do it with Zaria and I would do it with Selena. That's as far as the discussion went. You never said anything about there being a time limit."

"And I never agreed to any of it," Selena snaps. "I'm not your wife anymore. See?"

She holds up her hand again. She hasn't worn her wedding ring since before she and I went out.

"This isn't right," Landon insists. "You stole her from me by force."

"You were more than happy to throw her at me," I tell him. "All of this was your idea, remember?"

"I never said anything about *this!*" His voice starts to rise. The other patrons turn around to stare at us. "You're a fraud and a thief! You took her!"

"You're the fraud, Landon," Selena mutters. "You lied to me on our wedding day when you said you would be faithful to me forever. You're the one who is in the wrong here."

He takes a step toward the table, slams both his fists down on it hard enough to make the cutlery rattle, and leans in close to snap in my face. "You won't get away with this! The cruise line has rules against this!"

"Really?" I ask. "What rules are those?"

He's making such a scene that the restaurant manager comes over to our table. The guy wears a white chef's apron over his big barrel chest and large stomach.

He takes hold of Landon's arm and tries to pull him away. "Please, Sir. You're disrupting our other diners. You'll have to take it outside."

Landon throws the guy off and tries to take hold of Selena's arm. "Come on, Selena. You're coming with me."

She yells out, tears her arm out of his grip, and rears back in her seat to get away from him. "I'm not going anywhere with you! Keep your hands off me!"

The manager tries one last time to reason with Landon, but he's losing his grip on reality too fast.

He lunges for me and tries to attack me. I straighten my arm to shrug him away, but he's coming too fast.

The manager tries to get to him in time, and right at that moment, a big, beefy hand grabs Landon by the back of the collar and tows him away from me.

It takes me a second to realize that the person holding onto Landon is Troy Nixon, the *Electric Emerald's* Chief of Security.

He drags Landon off the table, shakes him a few times to make him stand up, and six other burly security guys step between him and our table.

Troy plants himself right in front of Landon. "You have a simple choice to make, Mr. Neise," Troy growls. "You can walk out of here on your own two feet.....or we can drag you out kicking and screaming like a little girl. I really don't care which it is. It's up to you."

Landon glares at Troy and then at us—and then Landon's expression changes when he looks up at Troy for the second time.

Only a certified, bona fide idiot would tangle with Troy. I can see that right now. The guy is an absolute fortress.

You wouldn't catch me messing with him. I wouldn't want him even looking at me like that or confronting me because I made a scene in public.

Landon gets the message loud and clear, tucks his head down, storms past Troy, and disappears out into the main concourse. Troy gives me and Selena a look and follows Landon out of sight.

The incident casts a silence over me and Selena. The manager, all the other restaurant staff, and the other diners go back to what they were doing. Selena and I continue eating our meal in silence. I don't feel like seeing a comedy act anymore.

Selena must be thinking the same thing. "Maybe we should go see some music instead," she suggests after we leave the restaurant.

"No, I think we should see the comedy. We need something to take our minds off what happened."

She looks around at nothing. "Are you sure? I don't know....."

I take her hand. "I'm sure. We don't need to slink off with our tails between our legs. We aren't doing anything wrong or anything we need to be ashamed of. I want us to get out in public and see and be seen. We have nothing to hide. Now come on. The show is starting soon."

Chapter 14: Selena

I roll over in bed and heave a contented sigh when I gaze through the windows at the ocean outside. I have nothing in the world to worry about.

Reese lies asleep behind me with his arm wrapped around my waist—or I think he's asleep until he pulls me toward him.

He growls under his breath, buries his face in my neck from behind, and sinks back into a deep sleep.

I'm too awake to go back to sleep, but I'm too comfortable to get out of bed. I pick up my phone and navigate to the room service menu.

I'm just deciding what to order when someone knocks on the door out in the living room. Whoever it is knocks a lot louder than the room service guy and I haven't even ordered yet.

The sound startles Reese into jolting upright. "Who is it?!" he calls out.

A distant voice drifts through the walls. "It's Troy Nixon. I'm the head of ship's security."

"Uh....." Reese scrambles to get out of bed. "Just give me a second...."

We both fall over ourselves getting out of bed and getting dressed as quickly as we can. "What does he want?!" I hiss under my breath.

"I don't know!" Reese whispers back. "It must be something serious! Maybe it has something to do with last night."

We both clamber into the first clothes we can grab. Reese pulls on his suit pants from last night, buckles his belt, and goes out to the living room like that.

I pull on a pair of casual slacks, clip on my bra, and pull a sweatshirt over my head. I don't have time to put on anything else or straighten my hair before Reese answers the door out in the living room.

"Hey, man," he begins. "What is this all about?"

"Do you mind if I come in?" Troy asks. "I need to speak to you—and Ms. Neise. It's important."

"Uh...okay." Reese stands back and holds the door open so Troy can enter.

He looks even bigger today. He isn't wearing a suit. He wears business casual khaki slacks, deck shoes, and a black polo shirt that shows off just how muscular his arms are.

He casts his usual all-knowing gaze around the living room suite and turns around to face us. "What do you want to talk to us about?" Reese asks.

"I'm here to investigate Mr. Neise's claim that you stole his wife by some kind of coercion or force." Troy's eyes dart to me. "He lodged a formal complaint with my office last night, which means I have no choice but to investigate. If I find out there was any criminal activity, the offender will be removed from the ship and handed over to the authorities of whichever territorial waters we happen to be sailing through at the time."

I groan, cover my eyes, and throw myself down on the couch. "I don't believe it!"

Troy raises his eyebrows at me. "What is this all about, Ma'am? Why is your husband making this accusation?"

"He's making the accusation because he's a jealous loser who is too much of a coward to face reality." I shut my mouth. "I'm sorry. I shouldn't be taking it out on you."

"I didn't take Ms. Neise by any kind of coercion or force—not at all," Reese explains. "Mr. Neise suggested that we do a couples swap. I would get together with his wife and he would get together with my girlfriend, Zaria. You can find her in suite 26A."

"So what happened?" Troy asks.

"The four of us met for dinner to see if we hit it off," Reese goes on.

"Actually, you and I met before that," I interrupt and turn back to Troy. "Landon cheated on me multiple times. He brought me on this cruise because he thought we could work things out. Then he suggested the couples swap and I knew it was completely hopeless. I broke up with him and told him it was over for good. I was sitting somewhere crying by myself when Reese came over. We started talking and he told me his girlfriend cheated on him, too. I told him about the couples swap idea and he said we should do it to pay the other two back for their betrayal."

"Then we met for dinner," Reese goes on. "Selena and I hit it off and Landon hit the roof. He got jealous, got cold feet, and tried to get her to back out of it."

Troy looks back and forth between us. "I'm guessing you didn't."

"We met up that night and decided to spend the rest of the cruise together," I tell him. "We both moved out of our suites and moved in together here. That's the whole story. There was no coercion or force. This is all just Landon's way of trying to tear us apart."

"Zaria can confirm that we planned to do the couples swap," Reese adds. "If you need someone else to confirm it."

"I see." Troy frowns to himself. "I will definitely follow that up. Thank you both for your time. I'm sure this will come to nothing, but I have to continue with my investigation anyway. I hope you understand."

"Of course." I stand up. "Thank you for coming to talk to us."

Reese lets Troy out of the room. We both sink onto the couch as soon as he leaves. "Wow," Reese breathes. "Landon is really going off the deep end."

"Can you believe this? Imagine him coming up with a story like that to get you into trouble. He must be really desperate."

Reese leans back, rests his hand on my neck, and rubs. "I want you to get out today. Go get a massage or something."

"What are you going to do?"

"I have some business I need to take care of back home. I have to make contact with my team at the company and I need to take care of a few things for my website. You don't need to hang around for that."

I spin around. "I want to see! I want to see what you do with your web business."

"Not now, baby. You can see all that later. I'll be in meetings with my sales manager and a few other salespeople I'm training. You don't need to be around for that. You would make me uncomfortable if you were just sitting around watching and listening—and most of it is confidential anyway."

"What about the website stuff?"

"I have to answer a bunch of emails, post some stuff online, and do some marketing work. It's boring. I'll make you a deal. When we come back here tonight, I'll put you on the website and you can read some of the content. I'm warning you. It's all about motorcycles. You might find that really boring, too."

"I don't care! I want to see what you're doing. This is going to be great!"

"I don't know about that, but you'll at least be able to see it." He stands up. "I'm going to take a shower and get dressed. Order breakfast for us. Then we'll go do stuff today."

He heads back to the bathroom. I get my phone and place the order I was going to place before Troy interrupted.

I can't believe Landon is really doing all of this to try to break up me and Reese. Landon is turning out to be a much bigger creep than I realized.

Chapter 15: Reese

I lean back in my chair and listen to my sales manager and two other salespeople from my company try to work out a problem that has nothing to do with me.

I could be spending this time with Selena. Instead, I'm stuck in a meeting.

No one is paying attention to me, so I pick up my phone and navigate to some of my marketing apps. I try to get some of my marketing done and answer emails while I wait.

I get pulled back into the meeting. One of the people involved is a guy I've been training for the sales team. He's having problems because he doesn't know as much as I do. He can't answer the customers' questions or talk to them the way I do.

He's considering dropping out because he doesn't think he's qualified to do the job. He gets progressively more agitated and upset the longer the meeting goes on.

I send him a text to stay on the line after the meeting ends so he and I can talk. I tell him I think I have some information that will help him.

It always happens like this. I only have to talk to people. They complain about gaps in their knowledge or bemoan that they have nowhere to go to get the information. The internet doesn't help.

All I have to do is suggest that they join my forum. They're always super excited about it and grateful that they can find a place to ask questions and get answers from such knowledgeable people.

The meeting eventually ends and I tell him about the forum. He practically breaks down in sobs. "Thank you, man," he chokes. "I don't know what to do."

"It's simple," I tell him. "Just go on there anytime you have a question. Anyone on there will be happy to help you out."

He thanks me again and we get off the call. I concentrate on my marketing and decide to take a walk around the deck while I finish my emails. I need to get out of the suite, too.

I go down to the pool, lounge in the sun, and then head inside to see what's on at the shows tonight. I want to take Selena out again. We both had fun at the comedy club. We should try something different tonight.

I stop in front of one of the music venues and read a list of the bands, acts, and open mics scheduled for later today. The acts start at two o'clock in the afternoon and run until after midnight.

I don't want to decide on anything until I talk to Selena about it. I sit down on a bench under an indoor palm tree and finish my marketing tasks before I stand up to walk away.

I plan to go find Selena. She should be done with her massage by now.

I'm not thinking about anything else when Zaria rushes up to me and grabs my hand. "Reese! I've been looking everywhere for you!"

"Well, you didn't need to. I have nothing to say to you." I pull my hand out of her grasp. Her touch turns my stomach. "You don't ever need to look for me again."

Her eyes well up with tears and her lower lip quivers. "I'm sorry...about everything....Please.....give me another chance.....I'll turn over a new leaf.....I just.....I can't live without you......"

I groan and roll my eyes to Heaven. "If you're so sorry, then you should understand why I can never take you back. You wasted my time while you slept around with anything that moved. Don't come crying to me about it now."

She bursts into loud sobs and attracts the attention of other passengers around us. "Please.....I love you.....You're the only man I've ever loved....." She grabs my hand again and actually drops on one knee in front of me. "I want to marry you....."

I yank my hand away even harder this time. "Are you out of your mind?! I would never marry you! I will never lay a finger on you again. Are you kidding me? You could be crawling with a thousand diseases! You are the last woman alive I would ever marry."

She starts to get to her feet when I pull away. "Please....Reese.....I'll do anything....."

"You're the one who did all this! What are you even talking about? You got exactly what you deserved. You know what? I really have to thank you for removing yourself from my life. Leaving you was the best thing that ever happened to me."

I turn my back on her to walk away, but right then, her sobs turn to choking sounds. Her rapid inhalations escalate. She gasps for air.

I turn around at the sound. Her hand flies to her throat and her eyes widen. She gets more and more frantic.

"Zaria?" I ask. "Are you okay?"

".....can't......" she husks. "......breathe......"

The other passengers who have been standing around listening to us argue all start whispering to each other and pointing.

Zaria's face turns bright red. Her eyes bug out of their sockets and then she topples right in front of me. She falls over on the floor, sprawls, and lies there convulsing, choking, and clawing at her neck.

I lunge for her and grab her. "Zaria!!" I yell. "Zaria!!"

She doesn't answer. She doesn't even see me.

"Someone call the medical team!!" I yell, but right then, the medical team rushes in and surrounds her.

I have to back off as a bunch of medics pull out all their equipment and start working on her. I can only stand aside and stare as they carry her away.

I'm still frozen in shock when Troy comes up to me. "What happened?" he asks.

"I….I don't know…..She was asking me to take her back and I refused. She got hysterical and started crying…..and then she fell over and started choking….."

He frowns to himself. "That's strange. It shouldn't have happened like that."

My head shoots up. "What do you mean?"

He shrugs it away. "I just never heard of anyone falling over and going into convulsions and choking from crying too hard—but you don't have to take my word for it." He points at the medics taking Zaria away. "They'll take her down to the infirmary. I'm sure Dr. McKinlay can explain everything to us."

"Um…..I don't know where the infirmary is."

"I'll take you—or we can just follow the medics." He studies me. "Are you still listed as her next of kin?"

"Uh….yeah." I run my fingers through my hair. "This all happened so fast. I guess I am. We didn't have time to change anything."

He nods like he's heard it all before. Maybe couples split up on the cruise all the time. I wouldn't be surprised.

"Follow me. I'll take you down there. I'm sure Dr. McKinlay will need your consent to treat her if she isn't able to give it herself."

We set off across the concourse. The medics are talking so loudly and all at once that I can't make out what they're saying. Zaria seems to be yelling the loudest, but she doesn't seem to be making any coherent sense, either.

They put her on a wheeled gurney and push her into the elevator. There isn't room in there for me and Troy, so we have to wait for the next elevator.

Zaria sees me standing outside and lunges off the gurney trying to sit up. She extends her hand and calls out my name, but the medics push her down and the elevator doors shut.

I feel uncomfortable around Troy when he's seeing my relationship fall apart in such a publicly embarrassing way. "I'm really sorry about this," I mumble. "I didn't mean to make this awkward for the other passengers."

"What were you doing when she came up to you before it all went down?"

"I wasn't doing anything. I was sitting on a bench checking my email. Then I got up and walked off to go back upstairs. She came up to me and grabbed me." I cringe and grimace in embarrassment. "She even went down on one knee and tried to propose to me in public."

He chuckles to himself. "Such a classic cheater move. They'll do anything to avoid consequences."

I look up at him. "Have you been through this before?"

"Me? No, I haven't gone through it. I've just had the misfortune of seeing plenty of other people go through it on the ship. Trust me. You aren't the first victim of cheating whose dumped partner tried to propose to get their loved one back."

I look away. "Well, it's the first time it's ever happened to me. I wouldn't mind if Selena proposed to me—but not her."

He laughs again. "Let's hope it's the last time."

The elevator doors open and we step inside. I really, really wish I wasn't spending all this time with him under such disastrous circumstances.

He's such an awesome guy. I really admire him. I wish I could get to know him without all this other garbage getting in the way.

Chapter 16: Reese

The elevator doors open in a much lower deck of the ship. It's ten decks below the concourse.

The hallway looks industrial with no frills, no carpet, and no decoration. Engine noise vibrates through the walls.

Troy leads the way down the corridor, turns through an open door, and walks into the ship's infirmary. It's a spacious, modern medical clinic with ten exam tables on either side of one big room.

The medics surround Zaria on one of the tables. She's going to pieces as never before, but all the medics look relaxed.

They go about their business and don't try too hard to fix anything about her. One of the female medics stands off to one side scribbling on her clipboard.

Another male medic coils up some wires attached to a machine. He opens Zaria's shirt and unclips the electrodes from tabs glued to her chest and ribs.

A young man with dark curly hair and dark eyes strolls over to us. He wears a knee-length white lab coat over a business shirt and pants.

Curly blue embroidery on his lab coat reads, *Dr. Cameron McKinlay, Emergency Medicine.*

He nods at Troy. "How's it going?"

Troy jerks his thumb at me. "Dr. Cameron McKinlay, meet Reese Shipley. He's Zaria's next of kin."

Dr. McKinlay nods to me, too. "There's nothing wrong with her. She hyperventilated. She'll be fine now as long as she doesn't start doing it again. If she does, you can coach her to calm down and slow her breathing. Some people advise putting your hand over her mouth and pinching her nose shut, but I don't think it's a good idea if you know what I mean."

"Hyperventilating!" I exclaim. "Are you sure it was only that? It looked like she was dying or something."

"She probably wanted you to think she was. Patients who hyperventilate this badly are usually prone to dramatic outbursts. Trust me. She's fine. Try to ignore the noise. She'll experience tingling in her extremities and tightness in her chest. Patients often mistake these as signs that they really are dying—which makes them hyperventilate even more. The absolute worst thing that can happen is that they'll pass out, but that will only cause their breathing to return to normal sooner. Sometimes losing consciousness is the best way to calm them down."

I stare at him in shock. "Really? I had no idea. What about the whole breathing into a paper bag thing? Does that actually work?"

He laughs. "It works, but you aren't likely to be walking around with a paper bag in your pocket the next time it happens, are you?"

I look away. "No, I guess not."

"Everything checks out. She appears to be perfectly healthy. We'll just keep her here until she calms down."

He wanders off to go do something else, and in a few minutes, Troy leaves, too. He has no more reason to stay.

I turn back to the exam table. Zaria lies there crying, howling, bellyaching, begging the medics to help her, and thrashing all over the place like she's in pain.

I look at her in a whole new light now. Here I was all worried that something was seriously wrong with her.

No doubt that's what she wanted me to think. What a manipulative witch.

Almost the instant I think that, she lunges off the bed and thrusts out her hand to me like she really is about to die a horrible death.

I hate her guts, but I can't stay mad at her. She's so unbelievably pathetic. How pathetic does a person have to be to pull something like this?

Someone on the ship could have been having a real medical emergency. The medics and doctors wouldn't have been able to help the person because they were too tied up with Zaria's hysterics.

I take a few steps toward the bed, but I make sure not to get close enough for her to touch me. That would be my worst nightmare.

Just then, Dr. McKinlay comes over to me holding out a tablet. "I just need to get your signature as her next of kin...."

"I'm not her next of kin anymore," I tell him. "We aren't together. We broke up a long time ago, but we'd already signed up for the cruise. Neither of us changed the paperwork. If you're telling me she's mentally competent, then she can sign for herself."

Zaria overhears me and flies into another emotional outburst. "No, Reese! Don't say that! I love you! We can work this out! I'll make a good wife for you....."

"We will never get back together, Zaria!" I snap. "Get that through your head! Not all the theatrics in the world will ever force me to get back together with you! I don't know how many times I have to say it."

She flops back on the pillow bawling her eyes out and howling like anything. Her voice echoes through the infirmary and down the hall.

I start to turn away. I don't need to be here for this.

I head for the door just as Selena comes in heading the other way. She looks back and forth between me and Zaria. "Troy told me you were down here. Is everything all right?"

"You filthy rotten bitch!" Zaria bellows. "You're a homewrecker and a tramp! You slut! You stole him from me! You don't deserve to walk around alive on this earth if you could do something like this to me! I hope you die, you skank!"

"Zaria—stop it!" I snap. "Everything you're saying about her is true for you!"

Selena goes ice cold, glares at Zaria, and stalks straight back out of the room.

I storm over to Zaria's bed. "How dare you talk to her like that?! How dare you call her a tramp and a slut?! If anyone is, you are!"

"She stole you from me!!" she roars.

"She didn't do anything! You brought this on yourself by sleeping with half the town! I broke up with you before I ever laid eyes on her! Pull your head out of your ass and act like an adult for once in your life! You're an embarrassment to the whole human race acting like this!"

She flops back on the pillow yowling to High Heaven. I can't help but notice Dr. McKinlay and all the medics watching and listening. Jesus, what a nightmare!

At least Selena isn't here anymore. No one is going to talk to her like that while I'm around.

Zaria carries on writhing on the bed in torment—or she wants me to think so. This is all an act. It probably would have worked in the early days. Now I see straight through her.

I wait a little while until she breaks down sobbing with her head turned all the way away from me.

I take a chance and sit down on the edge of the bed. I don't touch her in any other way. I don't want to give her the wrong idea.

"It's over," I murmur under my breath. "What we had will never come back. You need to pull it together and move on. I'm sure you can find someone else to take your mind off me."

"No!" she moans. "I don't want anyone else but you!"

"You want everyone else but me. You never wanted me. You just wanted a boyfriend while you played around with everyone else who would look sideways at you. You never wanted me."

She really starts crying then. Of course it's true. I was never more than a window dressing to her.

"Don't let me see you around Selena again," I mutter under my breath. "Don't come around me trying to get me back. It's over. Don't go telling anyone she stole me from you because we both know that isn't true. I'm doing you a favor by not broadcasting it all over social media what you really did to me. I'm sure if I post your picture online, we can find all kinds of guys who will come forward to say they hooked up with you. Just be grateful to leave it alone and move on. That's what I'm doing. It's the civilized thing to do. Don't make it worse than it already is."

I stop there, stand up, and leave. I can make this a whole lot more unpleasant for her if she really wants me to.

I can be the bigger person and leave it alone. That's what I want. I just want to move on with Selena and forget Zaria even exists. If she doesn't, she's going to find out I'm not the nice guy she thought I was.

Chapter 17: Selena

I walk out of the elevator still fuming about all the nasty names Zaria called me. I should have known better than to go down to the infirmary to check on her.

How dare she call me a slut and a homewrecker? Reese is right. She's the pot calling the kettle black.

It still burns me up inside. I need to calm down.

I walk down the breezeway heading for the pool. The sea air blowing in my face and hair helps cool me off, but it also raises so many questions in my mind.

What if Reese makes up with her? What if her tears actually sway him to go back to her?

Why is he even in the infirmary with her when they aren't together anymore? What do I really have with him besides a whole lot of sex and a few dinner dates?

I should just go home and start arranging my affairs to divorce Landon. I should take advantage of the time while he's here so I can get a jump on things.

I shouldn't put so much stock in Reese. He's a nice guy and we have a nice time together, but it isn't like we could ever build anything long-term—not based on such a spontaneous hookup.

Leaving the cruise early will probably get complicated. We're making our first port of call tomorrow. I can do it then.

Then I won't have to worry about the crew bringing in a chopper to fly me out. That isn't necessary when tomorrow will work just as well. I can fly out of the airport instead.

I make it halfway to the pools when Landon steps out in front of me.

He gives me his heartbroken look. "Do you mind if we talk for a minute?" he asks in a choked undertone. Is he about to start crying?

I shrug. "Fine. What do you want to talk about?"

"I'm....I'm really sorry....about everything....."

I snort at him. "Something tells me you aren't."

"I'm trying to do the right thing here!" He gulps. "I'm sorry....that I hurt you.....and I'm sorry I made a scene last night at the restaurant. That was wrong of me."

I purse my lips. I don't want to talk to this idiot at all.

"I know I messed up," he croaks. "I know everything wrong with our marriage is my fault. I'm not a good person if I could do something like this, especially to someone as good as you. You treated me so well and I....I betrayed you."

"Well, at least you finally realize that." I try not to snap at him, but it comes out that way anyway.

He flinches like I just slapped him. "I do realize it. I just want.....I just want things to be......maybe not friendly, but at least civil. I want us to at least be able to have a decent conversation....and work things out.....and figure out what we're going to do with the house and everything....Can't we at least do that?"

I heave an exasperated sigh. "All right. If that's all we're doing, I guess we can. Why don't we sit down somewhere?"

I wave toward the concourse. We go in there and sit down on a padded bench in a quiet corner. We both lean back and turn to each other.

"So what do you want to do about the house?" I ask. "Do you want to keep it or sell it?"

"I want to keep it. I'll buy you out of your share."

"Good. That part is settled then. I'll remove my name from our joint bank account and open a new one. I can transfer my salary into the new bank account so you don't have to worry about that."

His features pinch and his eyes water again when he looks at me. "I'm really sorry about this."

"You can stop saying that. Let's just get through this and handle our business so we can both move on in different directions."

"No, I mean it." He thrusts out his hand and squeezes mine. "You're such a good person. I never deserved you. I was never good enough for you."

I pull my hand out of his. "Try being a better person in the future and we'll call it square. You can pack up all my belongings in the house if I don't get there first. I don't care about any of it."

"What about your art supplies?" he asks. "You need those for work."

"I can replace them all—but if you really don't know what to do with them, you can either pack them up yourself or leave them alone and wait for me to do it. It really doesn't matter."

"I wish…." He looks away. "I wish things could be different between us."

I can see this turning into another emotional trip down memory lane, so I change the subject. "What do you want to do about the cars? They're in both our names."

"Why don't you take the Toyota? I'll take the Chrysler. We can both sign over the other car."

"Great. Is there anything else we need to work out?"

"I don't think so. If anything comes up, we can discuss it later, right?"

"Okay. I'll see you around. I'll text you when we get back to town about when will be a good time for me to come and pick up my stuff."

I walk away. I don't want to talk to him ever again, but I guess I have to until I untangle my life from his.

I make up my mind right then and there. The minute I get back to town, I'll go to the art supply store and buy replacements for all my supplies that I left behind in that house. I don't want him holding that over my head.

I'll use up the new supplies pretty soon anyway. None of that stuff will go to waste. Then I'll have enough to work with until I can clear out his house.

It's his house now. I don't want it. I never want to see it again.

I don't know what I'll do with the money I get from the sale. I'll have to think about that.

I'll have enough time to decide where to live when I get back to town. I'll also have enough time to buy my new art supplies after I get back to town ahead of him.

That extra time is going to be important. I want a cushion between when I get back to town and when I have to deal with him.

I want to establish myself in my own right. I want to start building my new life apart from him. I need that time to do it.

I need to clear my stuff out of Reese's suite, too. I need to break the news that I'm leaving early. I don't want this uncertainty hanging over my head that he might get back together with Zaria. I don't need that.

Chapter 18:
Selena

I take the elevator back upstairs and let myself into the suite. I see him leaning against the kitchen counter with his arms crossed over his chest.

"How's Zaria?" I ask.

"She's fine," he clips. "How's Landon?"

I spin around in surprise. "What?"

"I just saw you two holding hands downstairs. Just come right out and tell me. You're getting back together with him, aren't you?"

"No, I'm not! How can you even think that?"

"Oh, I don't know. Maybe because I just saw you cozying up with him in an intimate setting...."

"I was not cozying up to him, Reese! We were talking about how we were going to divide up our assets and deal with the house. He was the one who got all emotional and tried to apologize to me for being an asshole. He squeezed my hand, but I pulled away immediately. If you were really there, you would have seen that."

He shrugs that away. "I didn't see that. I saw you and I walked off. If you're going back to him, go ahead and do it. Don't string me along."

I throw up my hands and snort. "You're the one cozying up to Zaria and being all comforting in the infirmary. Why don't you go back to her?"

"I was not cozying up to her and I was not being comforting! I told her we would never get back together!"

"You deal with your own crap, okay?" I turn and head for the bedroom. "I'm leaving the ship tomorrow to go home. I don't need this."

He doesn't follow me—not for a minute. When he does, he storms into the bedroom and stops next to me. I'm already standing at the dresser getting ready to organize my stuff to pack into my suitcase.

"What do you mean—you're leaving the ship tomorrow?" he asks.

"Look. You don't trust me not to go back to Landon and I don't trust you not to go back to Zaria. We had a nice time together and we both helped each other move on. I'm grateful to you for that, but I need to get my life together. I can't do that here and I can't do it with you. I need to start rebuilding before I can look around for someone to start a real relationship with. That's never going to be you."

I turn my back on him, get my suitcase out of the closet, and open it on the bed. He stands there watching me for a long moment of silence before he breaks it.

"Are you seriously telling me you would never get back with Landon?"

I roll my eyes at him and start getting my clothes out of the closet. "You don't know me very well if you could even ask that. Are you seriously telling me you would never get back with Zaria?"

"Of course not! She disgusts me. I only went down there because I'm still listed as her next of kin on the cruise line paperwork—and I told the doctor that I wouldn't sign for her because we aren't together anymore. You weren't there. You didn't hear what I said to her after you left. It's over. I will never go back to her even if you do leave tomorrow."

"Well, you weren't there, either. You didn't hear what I said to Landon and you obviously didn't see me pull my hand away from him. He disgusts me just as much. I wouldn't go back to him no matter what happens with you."

He comes over to me. "Don't leave. We can work this out and finish the cruise."

I don't stop packing. "I can't. I need to set up a place for myself to live, buy some replacement art supplies, and establish an independent life before Landon comes back to town."

"Can't you do all of that from here? Can't you rent an apartment, buy your art supplies online, and finish the cruise?" He dives forward, grabs my hand, and turns me around to face him. "Selena.....don't leave. I'm serious. This was just a little misunderstanding. You don't trust me not to go back to Zaria and I don't trust you not to go back to Landon, but we'll never build that trust if we bail out now. Stay. Let's decide to trust each other—at least until we have some reason not to."

I do my best to snort at him again, but it doesn't come out very well. "I don't need a reason not to trust you."

"And I don't need a reason not to trust you. Neither of us will find the relationship we want if we don't trust again. That has to start right now. This could be that relationship. I've never believed in anything as much as I believe in this—and I know you feel the same way. That's why we're both walking on eggshells. Give it a chance. Don't kill it over a little miscommunication."

I don't want to let my guard down with him again. I can't feel this way about him if I'm only going to get hurt again.

He takes the hint, puts his arms around me, hugs me, and pulls me down to sit on the bed next to him.

"Tell me everything that happened between you and Landon," he murmurs low. "I want to know everything."

I sigh and try to wave that away. "I was really pissed off because of everything Zaria said....."

"She had no right to talk to you like that. I told her off as soon as you left."

I hold up my hand. "It doesn't matter. I don't want to think about it anymore. Anyway, I started questioning everything with you and he came along acting all apologetic and weepy."

"Weepy!" he exclaims. "Seriously?"

I groan and roll my eyes to Heaven. "He's pathetic. Anyway, he said he was really sorry he hurt me and betrayed me and he knows he isn't a good person and everything that happened is his fault and all that crap. He said, if we can't be friends, that we should at least be able to have a civil conversation about how to straighten out our affairs. I knew we were going to have to have that conversation eventually, so I said okay and we went to sit down so we could talk."

"Okay, so you talked about your house and everything?"

I nod. "He's going to keep the house and buy me out. We're each going to take one car and sign them over to each other. I'm going to arrange a time to go over there and take all my stuff out of the house—which is why I have to buy all my new art supplies and everything."

He frowns. "I don't understand. Why do you need to buy new supplies?"

"Because I don't know when he'll be available for me to go get my stuff. I'll need to work until then—and it isn't like the supplies will go to waste. I'll use them eventually and then I'll have to buy more."

"Oh, I see."

I sigh and look away. "I really was looking forward to having that time in town by myself before he comes home."

He clasps my hand. "Let's go out to dinner again tonight. We need to spend some time talking to get closer to each other."

I look up into his eyes—and see all the memories of the last few days written there. I remember now why I'm so drawn to him.

He feels the same coldness and distance between us. He's having the same problem letting his guard down. He doesn't want to get hurt again.

My shoulders slump. "I'm sorry I doubted you."

"Don't be. I did exactly the same thing." He hugs me around the shoulders and kisses the side of my head. "What's happening between us is too important to throw it away like this. If there can be anything between us, I want to find out for real. I don't want some stupid misunderstanding to ruin it."

He stands up and crosses the room to take off his watch and put his phone and keys on the dresser.

I turn around and start unpacking my suitcase. "I guess I can put all of this stuff away."

"Don't you want to know what happened with Zaria?" he asks.

"You just told me. You said you told her off after I left and made it clear that you wouldn't get back together with her."

"I mean before that. Don't you want to know how she wound up in the infirmary in the first place?"

My head shoots up. "How did she?"

"She ambushed me in the concourse, started crying, begged me to take her back, and went down on one knee and proposed to me."

I blink at him in disbelief. Then I burst out laughing. "No way!"

"I told her she was the last woman alive that I would ever marry, that I would never touch her again, and that she could be crawling with all kinds of diseases from all the guys she's spread her legs for."

I gasp out loud. "You said that?!"

"Well, I didn't say the part about her spreading her legs, but I did say the rest. Then she started hyperventilating, fell over, and started choking on her own.....whatever the hell you call it."

I can't stop staring at him. "Wow. That's incredible."

"The doctor said she was fine and that it's normal for people who are hysterical and desperate for attention. Troy even said he's seen it before and he's also seen the whole cheater-goes-down-on-one-knee-to-get-their-loved-one-back thing."

I laugh again and cover my mouth. "Sorry! I know it isn't funny."

"I'm glad you can get some enjoyment out of it."

"I'm just amazed she went that far."

"Which one—the falling down and choking or the proposal?"

"All of it." I laugh again. "I really wish I had been there to see it."

He snorts. "No, you don't."

I chuckle and go back to putting my stuff away. "Wow. I really got off easy compared to you."

"I'm really sorry you had to hear her call you those names. That was totally uncalled for."

I glance at him and everything changes when I see his eyes. He's the one I've been having all these amazing experiences with. He's the one who has always been there for me.

I go over to him, slip my arms around his waist, and cuddle into his chest. "Let's forget it."

He kisses me on the hair. "Does that mean you're ready to see a musical tonight? *Grease* is playing at the Allenton Theater."

I burst out laughing, rock my hips from side to side, and sweep my hand across the room. "Go, Greased Lightning, you're burning up the quarter mile!"

He cracks up and holds his hand in front of his eyes. "Aargh! I'm blind!"

We both laugh and I put the rest of my clothes in the closet. "Hey, let's go see it and call it a comedy act."

"You got a deal."

Chapter 19: Reese

I sidle up behind Selena where she's putting on her jewelry in front of the bedroom dresser mirror.

I slide my hands around her waist and the temptation becomes overwhelming to grab her hips, bend her over, and run my hands up her thighs under her short dress.

I lean in close and growl in her ear. "Do we have time for one last quickie before the show starts?"

She giggles and shoves her ass back against my hard package. "It's never a quickie with you."

"I don't hear you complaining." I slip my fingers between her legs and feel her panties already wet. "Holy crap, baby. I have to have you right this minute."

"Then there's no point going to the show, is there?" She squirms around to face me and plunges her hand between my legs to stroke me through my pants. "I could promise to give you a blowjob during the musical."

"You better not. We would get thrown out of the theater."

She breaks away laughing. "Then I'll promise to give you one when we get home. Come on. We're going to be late."

I have to adjust myself in my shorts before I walk out of the room. She really knows how to tease me.

She gives me a few blushing smirks in the elevator. The feel of her soaking wet panties drives me insane, but I have to pay attention when we get to the concourse.

I steer her to a different restaurant—a high-class gourmet one with an open kitchen right there in the middle of the dining room.

This restaurant is noisy, busy, and everyone in here is dressed up to the nines.

She's beaming from ear to ear when we sit down at a table where we can see the chefs doing their thing. We order drinks and then appetizers.

She has to yell over the noise. "This is awesome! I love this kind of thing! It's like another kind of theater."

"Did you ever want to be a chef?"

"No, not in a restaurant where the patrons can complain about my food. I did like cooking for Landon, though."

My head shoots up. "You cooked for Landon?"

"All the time. I did all the cooking the whole time we were together."

"Was he no good at it?"

"I don't know why. Maybe because I enjoyed it and I liked cooking for him. I liked making him happy that way."

I slip my hand across the table. "Would you like making me happy that way?"

Her smile slips and her hand goes cold in mine. "You and I both know nothing is going to happen between us after the cruise. This is just a nice time before we both go back to real life."

"Is that all it is?" I ask. "A nice time?"

She grimaces and looks away. "I don't want it to be, but wanting it to be one thing won't change what it actually is."

"You said that in the room. You said I could never be the person you build a real relationship with."

"Well, think about it. You live on the other side of the country from me. How would we ever be together?"

I shrug and wind up squirming. "I don't know, but I'd like to think it was possible."

"How could it be possible?"

"Just tell me you would like to think it's possible, too. Tell me that's the only reason you don't think we could ever be a real couple."

Her face spasms. She looks like she's about to burst into tears. "Of course it is," she croaks.

I raise her hand and kiss the back of her knuckles. "All things are possible if we only want them badly enough."

She bites back another pained expression, but right then, we hear an outburst of loud voices nearby.

We both turn and my world stops when I see Landon again. He stands at the counter talking way too loudly to a bunch of other men. I don't know them, and from what I can see, they don't know Landon, either.

He holds a drink in one hand and sways while he blasts his too-loud voice into their faces. He's drunk off his ass, slaps them too hard on their shoulders, and almost falls over one of the guys when Landon tries to walk down the counter.

The guys give him strange looks. The other patrons notice and give him strange looks, too.

"Let's leave," Selena murmurs. "I don't want to be here."

I stand up. That's the moment when Landon sees me. He slurs his words and his knees bow when he yells across the room. "Hey! Hey, man! It's good to see you!"

I take hold of Selena's hand to lead her out of the restaurant, but it's too late.

He blunders toward us, trips over another woman sitting there, and staggers trying to catch his balance.

He lurches forward too fast, falls, and crashes down right on top of our table in front of Selena. I grab her and yank her out of the way before he hits the floor with the table, our drinks, and all our food landing right on top of him.

Selena screams and so do a bunch of other patrons. I pull her farther away as he flounders down there trying to straighten himself out.

A bunch of other patrons back away, too. Everyone at the counter turns around to stare at him.

He tries once to push himself up and falls flat on his face in the mess again. I'm just about to step in to do something about this when Troy and all his security guys show up.

They collar Landon and drag him off the ground, but he's too drunk to see straight—or I wish he was.

He turns around and leers at Selena cowering in my arms. "Hey, baby! You look fantastic tonight!"

Troy raises his eyebrows between him and us. "Was he bothering you again?"

"No, he was just drunk....but he was on his way over to our table when he....."

Before I can get the words out, Selena wilts in my arms. Her head lolls back and her knees buckle so fast that I lose my grip on her.

She topples across the floor with her eyes closed. "Selena!" I yell and drop on my knees next to her. She doesn't respond when I shake her. "Selena!!"

Landon tries to fight his way out of the security guards' hold. "Hey! That's my wife, you bastard!"

Troy steps between us again. "Back off, man."

"That's my wife!!" he bellows. "You get away from her!!"

I barely hear him. I try to get some response out of Selena—and then she starts shaking all over.

She doesn't open her eyes. She doesn't choke or sob like Zaria. Selena just spasms all over and her teeth roll back from her teeth.

Troy moves in and pushes everyone out of the way. "Stand back! Stand back, Reese! I'm calling the medical team!"

He actually has to drag me away from her and restrain me while he calls the medical team to come and get her.

Landon keeps blaring the whole time about how she's his wife and he insists on going with her. Troy gives me a disgusted look. "I have to let him come. He is her husband and he's her stated next of kin."

I have to bite my tongue when the security guys manhandle his drunk ass down the elevator with me and Troy. Alcohol fumes billow off him. He keeps repeating over and over all the way down there that she's his wife.

"It isn't like he's mentally competent to make medical decisions on her behalf, is it?" I mutter to Troy out the side of my mouth.

"This is a life-threatening emergency. The medical team doesn't need anyone's consent to take any measures to save her life."

I force myself to look away. "I better not find out anyone did anything to her."

"Hey!!" Landon bellows. "That's my wife!"

"No, she isn't," I fire back before I think to stop myself.

He charges me and the security guys have to restrain him.

"Don't do that," Troy tells me. "He's out of his natural mind."

"He's out of a hell of lot more than that," I mutter, but just then, the elevator opens.

We walk down the hall to the infirmary. The medical team is working non-stop on Selena. Landon tries to tell them that she's his wife, too, but they completely ignore him.

Dr. McKinlay is right there in the middle of it this time. He yells orders at everyone. The medics are so busy shooting her full of drugs, sticking tubes down her throat, and doing every other thing to her.

My stomach tightens watching this. Nothing better happen to her. I can't lose her.

How have I spent the last few days building such an amazing life with someone I just met? She's everything I dreamed of in a woman. I can't let her go—especially not like this.

Landon yells, "Hey! That's my wife!" again. Troy completely ignores him.

Something in the tone of Landon's voice makes me look in his direction. He sounds different.

When I look, I see him glaring straight at me. He isn't telling the security guys or the medical team that she's his wife. He's telling me—like I don't already know.

"You keep away from her!" he bellows. "You shouldn't even be here! You're nobody!"

Troy turns around and goes over there. "Okay, pal. I think it's time for you to go back upstairs."

Landon makes another surge against the security guards as they start to pull him away. "She's my wife! You're nothing! You're nobody! Hey! Knock it off! I'm her husband! That's my wife!"

Troy gets in his face to push him out of the room even though the security guys are already taking him there.

Without warning, he throws them off, breaks away with unnatural strength, and veers around Troy. Troy makes a dive for him and catches him around the waist.

Landon loses his footing, starts to fall, and makes one last dive to slam his fist into my face full force.

He flattens me, and before I know what hit me, he leaps on top of me swinging for the fences.

I raise both arms in front of my face to protect myself. He's so shit-faced that he doesn't even notice. He flails his arms in all directions trying to punch me before the security guys haul him away by main force.

Chapter 20:
Selena

I pry my sore eyes open and squint into the glaring overhead lights. I try to look around and see Reese sitting on the edge of my bed. His lips spasm and he fights to control his features. "Hey, baby," he husks.

"What.....what happened?" I stammer. "Why....where am I?'

"You're in the infirmary on board the *Electric Emerald*. You had a medical emergency. You've been in here for twenty-four hours."

I frown up at him and notice dark bruising around his eye. "What happened to you?"

"Never mind about what happened to me. The important thing is that you're okay. The doctor says you're going to make a full recovery."

"What happened to me?" I sink back on the pillow. "I feel terrible."

"The doctor won't tell me what happened to you. He says we have to wait for Troy to come downstairs first."

I furrow my brow trying to think. "Troy....the Security Chief?"

Reese nods. "I don't know why. I think there might be something weird going on."

I look around again, but there's nothing to see. "I don't remember anything."

"Do you remember Landon falling onto our table in the restaurant?"

I blink at him. "He what?"

"What's the last thing you remember?"

I open my mouth to answer, but right then, Troy Nixon walks in. He looks absolutely furious, but not at us.

He stops next to my bed. "Welcome back, Ms. Neise," he mutters. "I'm so glad you made it. I was really worried."

"We all were," Reese adds. "The doctor wasn't sure you would make it, either."

"What's going on?" I ask Troy. "Why won't anyone tell us anything?"

"I'm about to find out myself." Troy walks away. "Wait here. I'll be right back."

He leaves, goes into the doctor's office on the other side of the infirmary, and comes back with the doctor.

He's a young guy with dark curly hair, dark eyes, and a long white lab coat. The name on the lapel reads, *Dr. Cameron McKinlay.*

"This is Dr. McKinlay," Reese tells me. "He's been taking care of you since you came in last night."

"What's going on, Doctor?" I ask again. "What happened to me?"

"You were poisoned, Ms. Neise," Dr. McKinlay replies. "Someone dosed your drink in the restaurant. You were poisoned with digitalis that was stolen from the infirmary sometime in the last three days."

"Oh, my God!" Reese exclaims.

"Zaria and Landon are the most obvious suspects," Troy adds. "And Zaria came down here as a patient in the last three days."

"She's the only passenger who did down here as a patient in the last three days," Dr. McKinlay adds. "She could have stolen the digitalis while the staff were out of the room. Landon Neise has not come in here—for any reason—not before Ms. Neise was poisoned. I don't see how he could be the perpetrator."

"There is the possibility that one of the staff stole the digitalis, but none of them had a motive to poison you," Troy adds. "They also wouldn't have opportunity. The suspect pool is pretty small, to be honest."

"What are you going to do?" Reese asked.

"I have to conduct a complete investigation before I can do anything. In the meantime, I'll give Zaria a formal warning to stay away from both of you."

"She should have been doing that already," Reese snaps. "I already told her to stay away from both of us."

"We have that conversation on security camera footage. She probably thinks she was pulling a fast one by staying away from you when she delivered the poison." Troy turns to me. "Your husband is flying off the ship tomorrow morning."

"Why?" I gasp. "What did he do this time?"

"He attacked Mr. Shipley—right here in the infirmary while the medical team was working on you."

"He got drunk in the restaurant," Reese tells me. "He made another scene, and when you collapsed, he said I didn't have a right to be here and he punched me."

"Which means his stay on board a Paradise Cruise ship is effectively terminated," Troy goes on. "Violence is strictly prohibited. The chopper will fly him to the mainland tomorrow where the authorities will extradite him back to the US."

I groan and fall back on my pillow. "Oh, wow! This is bad."

"Not as bad as someone poisoning you with drugs stolen from the ship's infirmary," Dr. McKinlay interjects. "I'm going to keep you overnight for observation. You can leave in the morning if you're feeling better. Just take it easy for a few days and try to heal up. Digitalis is a powerful chemical that can cause major problems. If you experience any symptoms at all, I want you to come back immediately."

I nod. "I will. Don't worry."

He and Troy leave. I sink back on my pillows. I want to talk to Reese about everything that's been happening, but I'm too exhausted. I pass out and don't wake up again until morning.

I wake up to find Reese still sitting next to my bed, but he's sitting in a chair this time.

"Don't you ever sleep?" I rasp.

He smiles at me. "I'll sleep after I take you home. Something tells me you're going to need a lot of rest."

I groan and turn my head away. "Has anything happened since yesterday?"

"I had to go to Troy's office to give a statement. I asked why Zaria is still on the ship if she's such a strong suspect for the poisoning case."

"What did he say?"

"He said he still hasn't completed his investigation and he still doesn't have any ironclad proof that she did it. He said he can't remove her from the ship without it."

I shrug. "I guess we have to accept that."

"I guess so. Anyway, he did what he said. He gave her a warning to stay away from us and that he'll be watching her. One slip and she's gone."

Dr. McKinlay comes out of his office just then. He and some medics come over and do a bunch of checks on me.

"You can take her home," he tells Reese. "Just make sure she gets plenty of rest and doesn't overdo it."

"I will," Reese replies.

Dr. McKinlay leaves and I heave myself out of bed. "I feel like shit," I groan.

Reese pulls a bag out from under the bed. "I brought you some clothes to wear home. I didn't think you wanted to wear the dress you had on at the restaurant."

He unfolds some of my casual pants and a comfortable T-shirt and sweatshirt. I feel bruised and weak when I pull everything on.

I hobble out of the infirmary like a woman three times my age. Reese reads my mind and puts his arm around my shoulders while we wait for the elevator.

I have to lean against him for support. I can barely stand up.

We ride up to the main deck where we have to transfer to another elevator. We're walking across the piazza when we see a black helicopter coming down to land on the deck outside.

Reese still holds me around the shoulders while we stand and stare at the chopper touching down. A bunch of the *Electric Emerald* crew hold back crowds of passengers all staring at it.

My blood runs cold when the security guys lead out Landon in handcuffs, march him through the crowd, and hand him over to a bunch of armed Police officers on board the chopper.

They pull him on board, buckle his safety harness for him, and they sit on either side of him while the chopper lifts off and flies away.

I stare after him. I can't believe he actually got himself thrown off the cruise. This is the absolute worst outcome I can possibly imagine for this cruise.

This is worse than us getting a divorce. He'll be facing criminal charges when he gets back to the US.

Was it worth it to sleep around with all those women? Does he regret it at all?

Losing me must be the least of his worries right now, but I'm too weak even to worry about that. Reese leads me to the elevators, supports me on the way upstairs, and lowers me into bed.

I collapse, completely drained. "I'm so sorry you have to go through all of this," I mumble. "I'm not going to be much good to you like this."

"You're perfect for me like this." He starts taking off my shoes and then undressing me. "Put your pajamas on and I'll order room service."

I drag myself upright to follow his instructions. "Don't order too much. I don't have much of an appetite."

He only smiles at me, sits down on the other side of the bed, and pulls out his phone. "I got you a surprise."

"I can't handle any surprises."

"You'll like this one—and it doesn't require any physical exertion on your part. You just have to lie there like a slug."

I snort. "Thanks a lot. So nice to know you're looking out for me."

He laughs, pulls me down on his chest, and picks up the TV remote. He switches it on and the opening titles for *Grease* start playing on the screen.

"Yay!" I cheer. "This is great!"

"I thought you'd like it."

We both settle down to watch the movie. I laugh when the "Greased Lightning" title starts playing. "You better be grateful I can't dance now."

"I'm sure you'll give me a performance when you start feeling better."

He pauses the movie when the room service guy shows up with the food. I'm already feeling better and I eat more than I thought I would.

We relax and watch the rest of the movie. I already know I'm not strong enough to do anything tonight, but Reese doesn't even mention it. He doesn't even try to kiss me.

He changes into his pajama pants and a T-shirt, cuddles in next to me, and switches off the light.

In a way, this was one of the best nights of my life, too. Everything is okay and I can just relax and enjoy myself with him until I feel better.

Chapter 21: Reese

I come downstairs while Selena relaxes in our suite. She's already started to feel better even though she doesn't have all her strength back.

I head for the pharmacy to buy her a few things. Then I stop by one of the concourse restaurants and reserve a table for us tonight. I want to take her out and pick up where we left off. I don't want to wait any longer.

I leave the store and head back to the piazza to catch another elevator when I almost collide with Zaria coming around the corner. She must have just gotten off the elevator.

She's dressed up way too slutty for this time of day. She wears a tiny bikini top and microscopic shorts that broadcast far and wide that she's that kind of girl.

She bursts into a flirtatious smile when she sees me. "Hi!" she chirps.

I glare at her and clench my teeth to stop myself from going off on her right here in public.

"I know what you did," I snarl. "You won't get away with it."

Her eyes fly open. "I don't know what you're talking about!"

"Of course you do. You know you're under investigation for poisoning Selena."

She scoffs in my face. "Selena again! You'll get bored with her and whatever is going on between you two will end as quickly as it started." She makes a face at me. "Good luck with that."

She flounces off toward the concourse—probably to go get another notch on her bedpost. I wouldn't be surprised.

I glare after her fighting down a surge of pure hatred. God, I wish I could find a way to prove she did it! She belongs in prison if she could do something as vindictive as that.

I shake it off and do my best to calm myself down on my way upstairs. I don't want Selena to know Zaria said anything about us.

That still raises the question. What will happen to me and Selena when the cruise ends?

If we go our separate ways and never see each other again, then Zaria will turn out to be right. My romance with Selena will end as quickly as it started.

I don't want that. I don't want it to end—ever—but what's the solution?

I don't have any answers and I don't bring it up around Selena. She's delighted when I give her the stuff from the pharmacy.

"You didn't have to do that," she tells me. "I could have called down and had someone bring it up."

"I want to." I kiss the side of her head. "If you want to get all independent, you can spend some time on your own tomorrow. I have to work on business stuff for a few hours."

She smiles at me. "That's okay. I need to get out of here and walk around the ship for a while. I want to see people and smell the wind."

"We have a balcony, you know."

She laughs. She's starting to look as healthy as she did before. "I'll be okay. I can walk around by myself without falling overboard."

"I know you can. I just want to make sure you're okay."

She leans against me. "So what show are we going to see tonight?"

"I was thinking music. We haven't done that yet."

"What kind do you like?"

"They have Irish dance music with dancers."

She explodes with laughter. "Are you going to participate?"

I turn bright red. "They would call security if I did."

"What else do they have?

"What—are you shooting down my suggestion already?"

"I just want to know the options."

"They have an AC/DC cover band—and *The Rocky Horror Picture Show* is playing tomorrow night."

Her eyes pop. "No way."

I grin at her reaction. "You want to do both, don't you? You want to jump to the left and do the time warp again. I knew it."

"Oh, hell yes! I am so there!" She scrambles out of bed and starts buzzing around the suite. "I have to start getting my props ready—and my costume!"

I lean back against the headboard, lace my fingers behind my head, and grin watching her get all excited about this. I don't even know which show she wants to go see—or if she wants to see both of them.

I'm down with either—or both. I love doing new things with her. I love how enthusiastic she gets to try anything she hasn't tried before.

I let her run herself down until she gets tired. She gets tired much more easily since the poisoning incident. Then she takes a nap and we go downstairs to have a quiet dinner by ourselves.

I can already see her losing steam. She won't be up for either show tonight.

I study her across the table. I don't know what's going to happen between us, but I'm really starting to dread the day the cruise ends.

I'm the one who said anything was possible if we only want it badly enough. She said the distance between us is the only reason it wouldn't work out.

What's not to hope for in that? If anything is possible, why can't it be possible for us?

I spend dinner talking and joking around with her, but my mind keeps spinning through my life back home.

I have a great life. I have a vast network of people, clients, customers, and suppliers I spend all day talking to about something I love. Am I really going to give all that up to move across the country for a woman I just met?

My family lives in my hometown, too. Am I ready to move away from them—for a woman? Is she really that exceptional? Couldn't I find another woman who would give me just as much as she does or maybe more?

I don't want to find out. That's the thing. I don't want someone else. I want her. I don't want anyone if I can't have her.

Chapter 22: Selena

Reese bends over and kisses me. "Have a nice time. Get a nice tan. You're looking a little pale."

"You did that, sonny," I tell him. "You're the one who keeps me locked up in here around the clock."

"I plan to keep you locked up in here around the clock some more, so you better go get your daily dose of vitamin D."

I laugh at him and leave the suite. He has some work to do and I want to walk around in the sun and wind. I have definitely been spending too much time indoors.

I ride the elevator down to the piazza and go out to the pools. The sun beats down and I feel my skin starting to glow again. The warmth feels amazing.

The ship feels different, now that I don't have to worry about bumping into Landon or even seeing him. He's gone.

He's going to have his own problems to deal with when he gets back home. I hope he feels humiliated enough to stay away from me.

I might have to get a restraining order if he comes near me again. I don't want to, but he just doesn't get the message.

Troy will back me up and give statements about the stuff Landon has been doing on the cruise. That will be enough to slap Landon with a restraining order if I really need one.

A bunch of kids, rowdy teenagers, and even some adults splash and make a huge noise in the pool. It's a little too loud out here for me.

A few of them cannonball into the pool and spray water on the surrounding passengers. I don't want that to happen to me, so I go back to the rear deck in the ship's stern.

I stand above the wake and smell the spray coming out from under the propellor. I like it here almost as much as I like standing in the prow.

Fewer people come back here and the ones who do like to keep it quiet. It's a nice place to think and just admire the beauty of the surrounding ocean.

I find myself smiling into the sunshine. It makes me feel good—and it makes me feel stronger. I'm starting to feel normal again.

I can enjoy having sex with Reese again even if I can't go all night like I used to. I'll get back into it. It's only a matter of time.

In fact, I think I'll initiate something as soon as we get back to the suite. He needs a reward for taking care of his business.

I still haven't gotten a chance to check out his website. I can't wait. Maybe I'll do that tonight, too.

I find myself grinning when I think about seeing him again. He makes me so happy....but all the old questions still nag at my mind.

Nothing can happen between us after the cruise ends. He has to stay where he is to do his job. His family is there and his work network is there.

I won't have the resources to move across the country—and I'm not even sure if I should.

It would be nice not to live in the same town with Landon anymore, but my whole family lives in my hometown. I don't want to leave them and I'm sure Reese doesn't want to leave his.

I turn back to the wake. Seagulls fly over my head screaming at something. I look up at them, and right then, someone walks up to me and says, "Hi."

It takes me a minute to realize the person is Zaria. I stare at her in shock. "Uh....hi. Do you want something?"

"Nope!" She grins at me. "I just wanted to say hi and see how you were doing."

I can't speak for a minute. Is this the person who stole a lethal drug from the infirmary so she could poison my drink? Did she actually try to kill me?

Reese's words come back to me. Troy doesn't have any solid proof that she did it. She wouldn't be here talking to me right now if he did.

Is that the reason she's asking how I am—because she wants to find out how I'm recovering? Or is she just concerned?

Zaria pretends not to notice that I'm too flabbergasted to answer. She turns to the ship's railing, looks down at the wake, and inhales a deep breath. "It's so beautiful here, don't you think? I love it out here."

"Yeah," I murmur. "I love it out here, too."

"It's too bad about your husband getting shipped out, isn't it? It's too bad the whole thing went south. He seemed like a nice guy in a harmless kind of way—and he is the one who proposed the whole couples swap. I'm sure he didn't expect it to end this way."

I find myself looking out over the ocean. "Yeah. I'm sure he didn't."

"I love how the boat is like a little fantasy land completely discon-nected from reality, don't you think? It's like all our problems are all back there on dry land and we're here in this world where problems don't exist. Everything is perfect here and nothing can possibly go wrong. It would be nice if the whole world was like this, wouldn't it? Then everything would be perfect."

I study her from the side. She's acting all friendly and interested, but her words tell a different story.

The boat isn't a fantasy land where problems don't exist. She brought her problems with her and even created a bunch of new ones—worse ones.

Landon did the same thing. His problems got a thousand times worse when he came onto the boat and so did mine. In fact, the same thing happened to all four of us.

She can't possibly believe what she just said. The boat is not a world apart from reality. It's a smaller slice of the same reality.

Maybe I'm reading too much into this. Maybe she can't possibly be evil enough to be the person who poisoned me.

"Anyway, I'm sure we'll all go back to our real lives when this is over," she goes on. "You'll go back to wherever you came from and your husband will still be there. I'll go back to my hometown and Reese will still be there." She levels me with a brutal stare. "Nothing will change."

The hair stands up on the back of my neck. I don't have to ask what she means.

She really believes that. She really thinks she'll get back together with Reese and I'll get back together with Landon.

Maybe she's right. Maybe Reese could never take me seriously and this is just a rebound fling for him.

Maybe he'll forget me as soon as the cruise ends. He'll go back to the town where he and Zaria already have a life. It makes sense that all four of us will get back together with the people we were with when we started.

I turn away from her. I have to get those thoughts out of my head. She keeps facing the wake, so I turn the other way. I need to clear my mind. I can't let her influence me to start doubting Reese and myself all over again.

I look up into the sunshine trying to get back that beautiful, happy feeling. That's the moment when I see Reese step out onto the balcony of our suite upstairs. He looks straight down at me and his mouth splits into a grin when our eyes meet.

His face turns black when he sees Zaria standing next to me. He clamps his lips shut tight and his eyes narrow in pure, venomous hatred.

He was telling the truth. He'll never get back together with her. He hates her—and why shouldn't he after she wrecked his life?

All the doubt evaporates from my mind. He loves me and I love him. What we have is real.

I don't need to know anything more. I turn back to tell Zaria that our conversation is over.

At that moment, she slams into me from the side, grabs me, and flips me over the side. I plunge straight down into the ship's wake and freezing cold water closes over my head.

Chapter 23: Reese

I stare in abject horror as Zaria throws Selena off the ship and she falls straight into the wake behind the boat.

I take a split second to realize what just happened. Then an explosion goes off in my mind. I dive for the emergency stop alarm next to the balcony door, slam my hand down on the button, and blast out of the suite heading for the stairs. I don't have time to wait for the elevator.

The emergency alarm howls through the ship as I charge down the stairs to the main deck. I have to push people out of the way before I burst onto the rear deck of the ship. Zaria isn't here anymore, thank God. I don't know what I would do if she was.

I look up at the bridge and wave my arms, but I can already see the officers and bridge staff pointing behind the boat and looking through their binoculars. They don't see me.

Selena is just a tiny black speck in the distance. The boat traveled a long way after she fell overboard, but at least she's still floating.

The ship's staff is already scurrying around the decks telling everyone to stay calm, but I don't care.

I climb onto the rail, dive off, and start stroking out there to get Selena. I don't even know if she can swim, but I have to help her either way.

I swim my hardest and catch up with her. She's treading water and holding herself up. "I'm here, baby!" I gasp. "I'm here! You're gonna be okay!"

"Reese!" she shrieks. "Zaria! Zaria....she pushed me over!"

"I know, baby! I saw the whole thing!" I swim up in front of her. "I don't want you to tire yourself out. You can hold onto me. I'll tread water for both of us until the ship sends someone out to get us."

Her frantic eyes dart around everywhere. "The ship.....it's so far away...."

"Look at me, baby!" I get in front of her. "I love you! I love you more than anything! I want you forever! Pay attention to me, baby! I'm right here! I'll always be here!"

Her cheek twitches. "I love you....I just don't know.....I don't know what's going to happen to us....."

I swim in close, grab her arms, and force her to put her arms around my neck. "I'm going to help you stay afloat until someone comes to get us. That's what's going to happen to us. That's all you need to know."

She clings to me and I hear her choking back sobs when she hugs me. "I....I don't know how much longer I can stay up."

"You'll be okay. I'll hold you up. Try to rest."

I want to hold her, but I have to tread water harder to hold up both of us. She kicks a few times, but her strength is already draining away. She rests her head against mine.

Nothing matters because I love her and she loves me. No one will ever take her away from me—not ever. Just don't ask me to make any decisions about the future.

I keep my back to the *Electric Emerald*. I don't want to know how long it will take for the crew to send out someone to come and get us. The captain and bridge staff might have to call in a rescue chopper.

I dig in to tread water all night if I have to. I want Selena to rest. If I get too tired, she'll have the strength to tread water for a while so I can do a dead-man float and regain my strength.

She's more important right now. I just want her to feel safe and supported. I don't care about myself.

I only have to keep it up for a few minutes before a motorboat putters alongside us. The crew is all wearing life vests.

I hoist Selena on board and the crew pulls her in. Then they drag me up, too.

I collapse in the bilge with Selena. I'm too exhausted to think straight, but at least we're both safe.

The crew sends down two stretchers to hoist us back on board the *Electric Emerald*. I don't even try to walk to the infirmary. The crew puts us on gurneys and the medical team works on me and Selena while they wheel us downstairs.

They put me on one exam table and her on the one right next to me. I turn my head so I can gaze at her across that space.

She does the same thing. I would really like to shut my eyes and fall asleep from exhaustion, but I can't stop staring at her.

Love overflows my heart when I look at her. She's the one. Now it's up to me to make it happen. I just don't know how yet.

The medical team takes our wet clothes off, gives us some warm hospital pajamas to wear, and loads us with electric blankets to warm us up.

The heat makes both of us sleepy and she falls asleep first. She's still worn out from the digitalis poisoning. This is the last thing she needs.

I'm still lying there staring at her thinking about a million things when Troy comes in. He takes one look at her and comes over to my bed. "How are you doing?" he asks.

"Zaria did it," I blurt out. "Zaria pushed Selena over the side. I saw the whole thing from the balcony of my suite. I'm the one who hit the emergency alarm...."

He rests his big hand on my shoulder. "I know, man. I know all about it. We already know which alarm set off the warning and we have security camera footage from the rear deck showing Zaria pushing her over."

"So what are you going to do?" I demand. "You have to do something!"

"Calm down, man," he murmurs. "Zaria is under arrest in the security office. She's awaiting transportation to shore by the Police. Then she'll get extradited. She'll never walk around freely on this ship again. You have nothing to worry about."

"I want to be there," I fire back. "I want to be there when they take her off the ship. I want to see that she really is gone."

"Of course, man. Of course," he murmurs. "I would expect nothing less. Just try to get some rest now. She won't ship out for at least another ten hours. Don't worry. She's locked up and she'll stay that way."

I don't want to relax, but just then, Selena stirs and opens her eyes. She freezes when she sees Troy standing next to my bed.

He tells her the same thing and then Dr. McKinlay comes along to tell us we don't need to stay in the infirmary anymore. He tells us we can keep our pajamas on and he releases us to go back to our own suite.

Selena and I drag our exhausted selves out of the infirmary. Fortunately, it's only a short walk to the elevator.

I wrap my arms around her the minute the doors close. "Don't ever get hurt again, okay?" I husk in her ear.

"I love you!" she whimpers. "You saved my life! I'll never be able to thank you enough."

I kiss the side of her head. "Just come home and get in bed with me. That's all the thanks I need."

We have to walk the rest of the way to the suite. Neither of us thinks twice about food, shows, sex, or anything else.

I pull the curtains to darken the room, we crawl into bed, wrap our arms around each other, and collapse.

I let out a shaky sigh when I feel her body against me. I don't have to worry about anything else. All our problems are over. I can finally shut my eyes and relax.

I don't have to look at her because I can feel her right here against me. I feel her breathing. I smell her hair.

Her arm lies over my chest and she squeezes me extra tight every time she remembers to check that I'm still here.

I drift off into a dreamless sleep. I don't want to be aware of anything else until I wake up in the morning—or maybe not until tomorrow afternoon.

I really just don't care anymore if I ever leave this room again. I don't care about any of the activities going on around the ship.

I'm only on this ship for one reason—to be with her. Nothing else means a damn thing.

I jolt wide awake out of a sound sleep when I hear a phone ringing somewhere. It isn't my phone, but it sounds extra loud. I can't sleep with it constantly jangling in my ear.

Selena murmurs in her sleep when I try to sit up. I can't see a thing. It's pitch black in the suite, which means it must be nighttime outside.

I can't tell where that noise is coming from, but it's too loud for me to ignore. I have to turn on the light so I can see.

Selena groans when I turn the light on. She rolls away from me so I can finally sit up.

It takes me way too long to realize that the sound is coming from a regular phone sitting on the nightstand right next to my head. I didn't realize until right now that the suite even had a phone in it.

This is an old-fashioned plug-in phone attached to the wall. It has a bunch of emergency information stuck to the front. That explains why I ignored it.

The phone keeps ringing and ringing and ringing. It doesn't stop. It takes me another eternity to realize why. Selena and I both fell into the water. Neither of us has a working cell phone anymore. Both of our phones went down yesterday when they got wet.

I pick up the phone and hold it to my ear. At least it isn't ringing anymore.

"Hello?" I ask.

"I need you to wake up and listen to what I'm telling you, Reese," a deep man's voice snaps in my ear. "This is Troy Nixon, the ship's Chief of Security. Are you awake enough to understand me?"

"Uh....yeah. I'm awake. What's going on?"

"Zaria escaped from the security office. She's at large somewhere on the ship, which means you and Selena are in danger. I need you to wake up, wake up Selena, and start taking precautions to lock all your doors and windows. My team is on its way upstairs right now. We have a key card to get into your suite. Don't open to door for anyone else. We'll be there as soon as we can. Do you understand me?"

"Yeah. I understand. I'll handle it."

"Good man. I'll see you in a few minutes."

I hang up, but I'm wide awake now. Zaria is on the loose again. I don't need to know anything else.

I flip over and shake Selena. "Wake up, baby. It's an emergency. Zaria escaped from the security office. You need to get up so we can be ready to meet the security guys when they come."

Selena jolts wide awake, too. She sits bolt upright in bed. "How?! How did she get away?!"

"I don't know and I don't care. Come on. Get up!"

I climb out of bed. Both Selena and I are still wearing the pajamas they gave us in the infirmary. I don't bother getting dressed all the way.

I go out to the living room, shut the balcony doors, and lock them. Then I check the main suite door and lock that, too.

I'm just going around the suite checking that there are no other entrances when Selena screams from the bedroom. I rush in there just in time to see Zaria burst out of the closet. She must have already been hiding in there. Don't ask me how she got into the suite.

It doesn't matter. She lunges for the bed. Selena has been sitting on her side with her back to the closet. Zaria rushes her holding a knife. Selena doesn't get up in time.

I charge into the room just as Zaria makes it to the bed. She jumps onto the mattress and slashes the knife down at Selena from behind before Selena can get away.

The knife slices through Selena's shirt. She cringes in pain as the knife gashes her back just as she stands up and dives away from the bed.

Zaria falls across the mattress where Selena and I were just sleeping in each other's arms. Will I ever be able to sleep in this bed again? Will I ever be able to sleep again at all without worrying about Zaria coming after us?

She immediately starts floundering to get up and go after Selena again. Zaria bares her teeth in an animal snarl and yowls in murderous fury. Dear God! What happened to her? How did she turn into such a raving psycho so fast?

I dive onto the bed, tackle her, and pin her under my weight, but the madness consuming her makes her a lot stronger than I expect.

She wrenches out from under me and swipes the knife at me at close range. I'm too close to her to get away.

The knife cuts me down and across my chest. I roar in agony and blood pours from the wound, but I'm too out of my mind with fury and desperation to stop now.

I dive on top of her, pin her under my weight to hold her down, and grab her arm. She shrieks in wild fury and makes another stab with the knife.

I'm not in a good position to hold her back with only one arm while I try to restrain her with the rest of my body and limbs.

She stabs me in the shoulder and clips the outer muscle of my arm. I bellow in her face. Selena screams again from the other side of the room. I really hope she doesn't come over here to try to help me, but she does.

She races to the bed, grabs Zaria by the wrist, and Selena uses both arms to wrench Zaria's hand away from me.

Selena uses all her strength to hold Zaria's arm down. Selena lies on top of Zaria's arm so Zaria can't move the knife around at all.

I don't have any trouble holding down the rest of her, and right then, twenty security guys storm the suite. They must have used their own keys to get inside.

They surround us, take the knife away from Zaria, and physically restrain her while Selena and I back off.

She screeches in wordless insanity while the security guys flip her over, zip-tie her wrists behind her back, and then restrain her ankles, too.

Troy stands off to one side and watches them literally carry her out of the room.

"You two better go downstairs to the infirmary so Dr. McKinlay can patch you up," Troy tells me.

"No way," I fire back. "We're going out on deck and we're going to watch her until the chopper comes in to take her away. Neither of us is going anywhere until she's gone. The medical team can treat us there if they absolutely have to—or we can do downstairs after she's gone—not before."

He only nods and claps me on my other, uninjured shoulder. "Okay, man. I understand. Go out on deck. I'll call the medical team and they'll meet you there."

Chapter 24: Selena

Reese stands with his arms around me while we watch the chopper come down to land on the tennis courts by the pool. We're the only passengers out here. The security team is keeping everyone else inside.

Reese and I have been standing out here for five hours waiting for this moment. The medical team showed up a long time ago, gave him stitches in the cut in his shoulder, and bandaged the other cuts on his chest and my back. The medics say those cuts aren't deep enough to need stitches.

The security guys carried Zaria here straight from our suite. She's been lying on the bare, flat deck with her arms and legs bound all this time while the security guys stand guard.

They keep their weapons drawn, but she can't get away a second time.

She goes through the whole process of screaming at them, yelling threats and curses, begging and pleading, and then sobbing, crying, and moaning in despair.

I feel so many jumbled emotions about her—rage, pity, disgust, and sometimes even compassion. What a mess her life is—and for what—for a bunch of sex with guys she didn't even care about?

How can a person go so wrong so fast? She's facing four counts of attempted murder—three against me and one against Reese.

The sun is already coming up by the time the chopper arrives. More passengers crowd the piazza windows to watch, but the security guys won't let anyone come outside.

They leave Zaria where she is until the chopper touches down. When the time comes, they don't even cut the zip-tie on her ankles so she can walk to the chopper by herself. Wow. They really aren't taking any chances.

The guys surround her, pick her up by her arms and legs, and carry her out there.

The Police come fully armed and bring a lot more personnel than they did with Landon. Four of them get out of the chopper so the *Electric Emerald* security team can lift Zaria inside.

She goes into another fit of yelling, screaming, and thrashing around when they lay her on the chopper floor in the back. I can't hear what she's saying over the rotor noise.

The Police personnel load back inside the chopper and surround her. They all take their seats fully armed and the security guys back away as the chopper lifts off.

It banks and flies off across the ocean. Reese and I stand in silence watching it. She's really gone now. She's still alive. She's still out there somewhere, but she can't come back to the ship—not now.

Reese leans over and kisses the side of my head. He doesn't speak. He's the one person alive who knows what I'm going through right now.

I just went through one of the most harrowing ordeals of my life, but I didn't go through it alone. He was there and he's here now. We share that. We always will.

I don't want to give him up. I don't think I can.

How can I give up the man I've come to depend on for so much? The heart connection between us is more than I ever imagined possible. I don't want to face the rest of my life without sharing it with him.

I fall against him, lean my head against his chest, and shut my eyes. I don't want to be anywhere else. I'll never feel this sense of safety and comfort anywhere else.

How can I even think of starting over with someone else? I already found the right person. I can't face losing him.

Troy comes over to us. He speaks in a soft undertone that doesn't match how big and intimidating he is. "It's over. You two can go back to your suite. I'll let you know if we need to do anything to follow up on this. I'm sure the authorities will get in touch with you both about pressing charges against Zaria."

He walks off with the rest of the security team, opens up the piazza, and the other passengers flood out. They all talk excitedly, but they don't notice me and Reese.

No one who sees us can possibly know what the two of us have been going through. Troy is the only person who knows and he isn't part of this.

Reese loosens his hold on me and takes my hand. "Come to the concourse with me. There's something important we have to do."

I don't question. I trust him completely. I trust him with my life.

We're both still wearing the bloody pajamas we had on when Zaria attacked us. I guess we'll change when we get back to the suite.

He leads me to the concourse and into one of the many electronics stores. We buy two new cell phones and go through a lengthy process of getting our phone numbers transferred to the new phones along with all the data from our old phones.

The process takes two more hours, but we finally finish and trade numbers with each other so we can keep in touch with each other no matter where we are or what we're doing.

He finally takes my hand and leads me back up to the suite. We change our clothes. It's almost noon.

The suite is a mess. I'm tired, but I don't want to go to sleep.

I sit down on the couch and Reese sits down next to me. He picks up the room service menu and places an order for both of us. I don't even care what he orders. I'll eat anything at this point.

He hangs up, extends his arm over the back of the couch, and traces his fingers through my hair to brush it away from my face.

His eyes speak volumes. I see the same questions, concerns, and desires warring in his mind. Neither of us wants this to end, but it will eventually.

"I love you," he murmurs.

"I love you, too," I murmur back. "What are we going to do about that?"

"We have another week before the cruise ends. Why don't we talk about that?"

"Okay. Let's talk about it."

His features pinch. "I want us to keep going after the cruise ends. Say you want the same thing."

"I do want to. The only question is how."

He shrugs at nothing. "One of us will have to move to where the other lives—or we'll both have to move to somewhere in the middle."

"It will cost just as much if we move halfway as all the way. Your family lives near you and my family lives near me. I don't see any reason why both of us should give that up."

"You're right. It doesn't make sense for both of us to uproot ourselves. Only one of us should do it."

"I can't afford to move across the country. I'll only be getting half the value of the house from Landon. That might not be enough for me to buy another one—and I don't know if I'll have to stay in the area for a while until the divorce is final."

He looks away, nods, and furrows his brow in deep thought.

"What's on your mind?" I ask. "What are you thinking?"

He opens his mouth to answer, but a knock on the door interrupts him when the room service guy shows up.

Reese tips him and brings the cart inside. "Let's talk about this after we eat," he tells me.

We stay there on the couch to eat. I don't feel like going anywhere else.

"Can you believe how out of her mind Zaria was?" I ask. "She almost didn't seem human anymore."

"I know what you mean. I felt the same way. I didn't recognize her. I don't know what happened to her. I don't know how she could go from proposing to me one day to trying to kill me the next."

"What do you think will happen to her?"

He shrugs again. "I guess, if she's smart, she'll plead guilty to the charges and go to prison." He shakes his head. "I can't believe I'm using that word in the same sentence with someone I was in a relationship with. I guess I never really knew her."

I slip my hand into his. "I promise I won't end up in prison."

"You better not. Anyway, I'll make sure you don't. I'll keep you locked up at home doing your art. I'll never let you go outside."

I laugh. "Except when we go on scuba diving trips, right?"

He grins at me before he takes another bite of his sandwich. We can talk about this and live the fantasy even though we both know it will never happen.

I just want to pretend for the rest of the cruise. I don't want to face the reality that Reese and I will ever part ways.

I want to rebuild my life with him. I want what we have now to keep going and for that to be the new life I build after this. I can't imagine anything better than that. I just don't see how it would even be possible.

I finish my sandwich and take a yogurt cup off the room service cart when my new phone buzzes on the coffee table in front of me.

"It's a good thing we got new phones," I remark when I pick it up.

I hesitate when I see the screen.

"Who's it from?" Reese asked.

"It's my dad. It must be important."

I switch on the phone and open a video call from my dad.

"I'm sorry to interrupt your vacation, sweetheart. I wouldn't call if it wasn't important."

"I didn't think you would. What's going on?"

"Anderson is in the hospital. He was walking down the street and he got run over by an out-of-control car. The doctors don't know how much longer he has."

"Oh, my God! I can't believe it!"

My mind turns a few somersaults. Anderson is my older brother. We've always been close.

I can't imagine what my family must be going through—and then I realize. I might lose my only brother and I'm halfway around the world.

"I understand if it isn't feasible for you to make it home in time....." my dad begins.

I shoot off the couch. "No! I'm on my way right now! I'll be there as soon as I can. I gotta go, Dad. I'll get on the first flight back. Just.......just don't let him go. Tell him I'm on my way."

His voice cracks with anguish. "I can't tell him anything, sweetheart. He's in a coma."

I can't listen to that. "I gotta go, Dad. I'll be there as soon as I can."

I hang up....and look around to see Reese staring up at me. "Go," he murmurs. "Don't look back."

I don't need to hear anything else. I charge out of the suite shoving my phone in my pocket. I don't even waste time taking the elevator.

I run down the stairs to Troy's office. He's the only person who can help me.

I blurt out the whole story and he gets on the phone to bring the chopper back for me.

Then I take off back upstairs to pack my stuff and make flight reservations.

I finish long before it's time to leave. Now I have no choice but to come face to face with Reese in the living room of our suite.

He struggles to control his lips when he strokes my cheek and kisses me. "Go home and take care of your family," he croaks. "I love you. I'll keep in touch with you and make sure you're okay."

I can only nod in numb shock. I can't be leaving him—not like this.

He doesn't say another word. There's nothing else to say.

He accompanies me downstairs and we wait in the piazza for the chopper to come. I wheel my suitcase out there, climb on board, and we fly away.

I go into a mindless stupor on the way back to the mainland. The chopper takes me straight to the airport where I have to wait another seven hours for my flight.

I spend the time on the phone with my family talking about my brother's condition. My mother, father, and sister are all in shock. I'm in shock.

I can't make the plane fly any faster. It's already late at night over there, so we hang up. Now I'm alone.

I sit there staring at my phone when I get another call. It's from Reese.

The video link opens up and he smiles at me. "How are you doing?" he asks.

I cover my eyes. "I can't think. I'm so exhausted from the last few days—and now this."

"You have a long flight. You can sleep on the plane. I'm sure it will be a whole lot sitting around in the hospital once you get there. You'll be able to catch up on sleep and no one will expect you to do anything physically demanding."

I force myself to look up at him. "I miss you."

"I miss you, too, but this is more important. Of course you have to take care of this. I'm not going anywhere."

I flinch. He isn't going anywhere. I am.

Just then, an announcement comes over the airport loudspeaker. "That's my flight. They're calling us to board. I'll talk to you later."

"Okay, baby. I love you. Sleep well on the flight."

We hang up. I have to get ready to board the flight and deal with all the other passengers and flight attendants and everything.

I finally settle into my seat and buckle my seatbelt. I guess it's a good thing that I have to turn my phone completely off for the flight.

The plane takes off and I fall asleep with my head against the window. I'm too worn out from the last three days even to keep my eyes open a second longer.

Chapter 25: Selena

I get off the plane, get into a taxi, and ride straight to the hospital. I don't even bother to put my suitcase anywhere. I wheel it straight into the ward where my family stands outside my brother's room.

I walk in and see my mom and my sister standing there with their arms around each other. Both of them are sobbing their eyes out.

My dad stands off to one side wiping tears off his cheeks. My mom bursts into loud, wailing sobs when she sees me.

She comes toward me with her arms out. "He's gone!" she howls. "He's gone! He just passed a few minutes ago! He's gone!"

I stand in stunned horror. I can't even hug her back when she puts her arms around me and stands there shaking with broken anguish.

My brother can't be gone. I can't have flown all the way back here only to arrive too late. He can't have died within minutes of me coming here to see him.

I can't move or speak or even think. My mom breaks away, hugs my sister while they both cry, and then my mom really breaks down when she hugs my dad.

I can't even cry. My brother can't be dead.

I have to face reality when I look into his hospital room. The person lying on the bed doesn't look anything like my brother.

A thick swath of bandages surrounds his head. A tube goes into his mouth and another goes up his nose.

Bruises and bloody cuts and scratches completely disfigure his features. I don't recognize him—or I don't want to recognize him.

I can make out enough to know it really is him. No one goes in there to try to revive him.

My family goes through a long, long period of crying and hugging each other. None of them thinks about leaving the hospital.

I don't want to be here, but I can't leave as long as they need me.

I'm just wondering what to do when my phone buzzes again. I check it and see a text from Landon.

He says he heard about what happened with my brother's car accident and offers to do whatever I need to help me get through it. Landon doesn't know yet that my brother is already dead.

I text Landon back in a numb trance. I tell him I want to make a time to get my art supplies and pick up the car. He says I can come anytime, and when I ask if he'll be there today, he says yes.

My family finally decides they shouldn't be doing this in the hospital. We decide to leave. My sister gives me a ride home—to Landon's house.

I haven't told my family about his infidelity and none of them knows anything about what happened on the cruise. Now isn't the time to tell them. I'll explain after this whole thing with my brother blows over.

I keep my distance from Landon, make a whirlwind tour of the house, gather up the bare minimum of my work supplies, and tell him I'll come back for the rest later.

I put my suitcase in the car and drive to my parents' house.

It's a whole lot of weeping, wailing, hugging, and crying when I get there. I sit on the couch, too stunned to think about anything.

While I'm there, I get another call from Reese. I have to decline it. I don't want to talk to him while my parents are around.

Instead, I send him a text telling him what happened.

I'm so sorry, baby, he tells me. *How are you doing with it?*

I can't think. I need to figure out where I'm going to stay tonight and I can't even do that.

Would you like me to set something up for you?

I stare at the phone. Is he really suggesting that?

He's on a cruise ship on the other side of the Pacific Ocean and he's offering to set up a place for me to stay tonight?

I don't want to believe it. I go through a flurry of confused responses. Should I tell him not to so he can enjoy the rest of the cruise?

If he feels about me the way I feel about him, he won't want to enjoy the rest of the cruise.

I would be too concerned about him if our positions were reversed. I wouldn't be able to enjoy the cruise because he wasn't there.

I finally text him back. *Okay. I would really appreciate that.*

He replies, *No problem. Anything you need, I'm here.*

I don't know what to say. *Thanks,* just doesn't seem to cut it.

I stare at the phone for a long time. My mom interrupts me by sitting down next to me on the couch and squeezing my hand.

She starts talking to me about Anderson, how great he was, and how close he and I were growing up.

She doesn't know the half of it, but I can't feel anything. I don't know if I'll ever feel anything again.

I'm still sitting there in a daze when I get another text from Reese. He doesn't send a message. He sends a link to a temporary apartment complex. The apartments rent by the week and he's rented one for two weeks for me to stay in starting tonight.

The link opens to pictures of a beautiful, spacious, modern apartment with one bedroom and a balcony overlooking a nice courtyard garden. The whole thing looks immaculate—and expensive. Did he really do this for me?

I stare at it for so long that my mom bends over to see what I'm looking at. "What's that?" she asks.

"It's nothing, Mom," I tell her. "It's just something for work."

That satisfies her. She doesn't argue when I text Reese back.

That looks amazing. Thank you so much. I really needed that.

I love you. I'll be waiting by the phone if you need anything.

Nothing else happens for the rest of the day. My parents have to go through a torturous process of organizing the funeral. It will be on Saturday.

I finally tear myself away at about seven o'clock in the evening. I tell everyone I'm really jet-lagged and I need to catch up on sleep. Everybody hugs me.

I drive across town and check into the apartment. It looks as beautiful in reality as it does in the pictures. I unpack my suitcase and put my art supplies on the table in the living room. I can work while I look out the window at the courtyard.

I change into my pajamas and get into bed, but something's missing. I call Reese. He's just waking up—or rather, I wake him up. It's early morning there.

He rubs his eyes. "Hey," he croaks. "You okay?"

"Yeah. I've been with my family all day. I'm at the apartment now and I'm just about to go to bed."

"That's good. Get some rest."

"What are you doing today?" I ask.

"I'll work on my business for a while. I have a few more meetings with company people and then I have to talk to my financial advisor and contact some people in my family. I'll probably be on the phone and the computer for most of the day."

I try to smile at him. "Fun times."

"I'm sure it's a lot more fun than what you're going through. Don't hesitate to call me if you need anything—and I mean anything. Do you want me to order your art supplies online so you can get back to work when you're ready? I know you planned to be gone for another few days."

"I don't need anything. I went by Landon's house yesterday to pick up my car, so I have everything I need to get started. Thank you, though."

"How did that go? Was he civil?"

"He was fine. He wanted to talk more, but I just had to grab my stuff and go back to my parents' house. My brother's death actually gave me the perfect excuse to avoid talking to him."

He smirks. "Milk it for all it's worth, baby."

"Have you heard anything about Zaria?"

"Only that she's being extradited back to the US. Paradise Cruise Lines has some kind of extradition agreement with the countries whose territorial waters the ships pass through. Anyone who commits a crime on board one of the ships gets tried in the parent company's jurisdiction, which is New York City. So she's being extradited there—which means she won't be going back to our hometown anytime soon. Even if she gets out on bail, she'll have to stay within the jurisdiction unless she gets specific approval from the court."

"Wow, that's great. Then you won't have to worry about seeing her again."

"I'm not too worried about it. Something tells me she won't be getting out of jail for a long time." He turns back to me. "How are you feeling about being back there in the same town with Landon and everything?"

I look away and shrug. "I guess I don't really feel anything about anything right now."

"That's okay, baby. That's normal. I'm sure all of this will take time to process. It would take time for you to process just the divorce by itself. Now you have all this other stuff to go through. I better let you get some sleep. I love you. I'll be thinking about you today. Sleep tight."

I say, "Good night," and we hang up.

I lie there in bed staring at the phone for a while before I turn off the light. I do love Reese and I'm grateful for his help and support.

What kind of a long-distance relationship could we have on opposite sides of the country, though? I don't think I want that.

Every conversation I have with him is stopping me from finding someone I could build a life with here.

I hate to break it off with him, but maybe that's the best thing for both of us.

Maybe he'll get back to his hometown and realize the same thing. What we have over the phone is just a shell of something that probably never should have existed in the first place.

Maybe Zaria is right and what happened on the *Electric Emerald* was just a fantasy that would evaporate the minute we got back to the real world.

It sure does feel like it now. Reese and everything we shared is all so far away from me. It keeps slipping farther and farther into the past. It will probably stay there forever.

Chapter 26:
Selena

I hug my mom for the hundredth time. "I'll call you later, okay?"

She pushes me back and peers at me. "Are you sure you're okay?"

"I'm fine, Mom. I'm going back to work tomorrow. I'll feel better after that. It's been two days since the funeral. I need to get back into normal life."

"I just don't like this whole thing about you moving out of the house. You and Landon have always had a good marriage. Now isn't the time to make rash decisions about things like that."

"I don't want to talk about it right now, Mom. I have my own reasons for moving out and they don't have anything to do with Anderson's death. We can talk about it later. I have to go. I'll see you soon. You have my new address if you need anything."

I kiss her on the cheek, hug my dad, and get out of there. I've been spending all my time with my family both before and since the funeral. I just can't do it anymore.

I drive back to my apartment. I really love the place, but I do need to look for something more permanent. I have an appointment on Friday to talk to my bank officer about using my credit from Landon's house to buy something new.

The only question is how I'm going to be able to afford to buy a house on one salary. I won't be able to afford something as big or as nice as I had with Landon.

I don't need anything big or nice. I mean I don't need anything big. This apartment is teaching me that. I would be happy with something small as long as it's nice.

I enter the apartment and go over to the table. I'm all set up and ready to start work tomorrow. I'm really looking forward to it. I feel energized to start my new life.

I lay out all my brushes, paints, pencils, rulers, and my tablet. I have all the information from my latest contract and the instructions from the client.

I love my job. It's one of the best things about my life. I can rebuild anything as long as I have that.

I open my tablet and scroll to some of the text from the book that the client wants me to illustrate. I can already picture what I'm going to draw.

I outline it in my head while I fold some clean laundry. I'm really enjoying this new life of mine.

I'm just getting ready to go sit on the couch and relax for a while when someone knocks on the door. I'm not expecting anyone.

I think it might be the apartment complex manager or maybe a maintenance man. I open the door and have to rearrange my whole picture of the world when I see Reese standing there.

"Um......what are you doing here?" I ask and look around. "Aren't you....aren't you supposed to be....like on the other side of the world?"

"I left the cruise early. I had some business to take care of." He glances around the apartment. "Do you mind if I come in? I would really like to talk to you."

"Uh.....okay." I stand back to let him in. I still find it difficult to believe he's actually here. In fact, I find it impossible to believe he's actually here.

He surveys the room before he turns to me. "I'm sorry I dropped in on you unannounced like this. I really wanted to see you."

"Um....okay. Why are you here? So you left the cruise early. Didn't you have to go home? Don't you have a job and everything?"

"I do have a job. I have a job here. I transferred to a different branch of the same company. I moved here because I want us to continue our relationship."

I blink at him in stupid disbelief. "You.....you what?"

"You said you couldn't move, so that left it up to me. I started my new job three days ago, but I didn't want to disturb you and your family until after the funeral." He looks around again. "I can go away and come back later if you aren't ready."

My jaw hits the floor. "You've been in town....living here....for three days....and you didn't tell me?!"

"I didn't want to intrude on the funeral. I knew you and your family wouldn't be ready to deal with all of that, so I waited." He frowns at me. "Are you okay with this?"

I have to concentrate hard just to get my mouth shut. "This is....this is insane."

"Why is it insane? I didn't want what we had to just pass away and become a distant memory. You said the distance factor was the only problem you had with us continuing. Do you still feel that way?"

"Of course, but.....I didn't mean for you to just drop everything and move across the country! That's insane!"

"I didn't just drop everything. I still have my web business. I still have a job I love and I still get to spend all my time talking to other people about what I love. I'm just doing it with all new people now."

"What about your family? You're on the other side of the country from them."

"We do have a thing called airplanes, you know.....and phones....and the internet. I can go back and visit them. It's fine. I want to do this. I don't want you to think about that. If you want to continue with me....."

"I do!" I blurt out. "I just didn't see how it would work."

"This is how it would work. I'm living in the same town with you. We can go out. We can spend time together. We can do everything we were doing before and more. Isn't that what we both want?"

"Uh....yeah."

He takes a step toward me. "Would you be interested in going out to dinner with me tonight?"

I gape at him with my eyes bugging out. "You mean.....like.....now?"

He bursts into a grin. "Yeah. Now—unless you're doing something else."

"I wasn't. I was just getting ready for work. I'm starting up again tomorrow—so if we do this, I need to get home and get a decent night's sleep tonight."

He won't stop beaming at me. "Understood. I swear I won't lay a finger on you."

I snort. "Tell me another one. Are we going somewhere fancy?" I look down at his clothes. He's wearing business casual. He could have come from anywhere or be going anywhere.

"I hadn't decided where we would go. I was waiting to see if you were even willing to go out with me again."

I make a face. "You should know better than that."

"I didn't want to assume anything."

Now I look down at my own clothes. I'm wearing casual clothes, too. "I guess we aren't going anywhere fancy."

"I don't care where we go. We can just go out for coffee if you want to."

"I already ate dinner, so.....are you hungry for dinner?"

"Why don't we go to a diner? Then you can get what you want and I can get what I want."

I find myself smiling at him. "Okay."

He escorts me outside and leads me to a huge, glossy black Hummer parked outside the building. "This?!" I exclaim. "This is your car?! This is what you drive around town?!"

"It's a company vehicle. I would never drive this otherwise."

I gasp in shock and stare at the car. "You mean....the company doesn't let you ride around on your motorcycle?"

He blushes. "That wouldn't be professional. The company likes to make an impression and I do sometimes have to drive clients and other executives around. They need to be comfortable." He opens the passenger door. "Are you ready to go?"

I can't answer. I hardly dare to believe what I'm seeing when I climb into the seat.

The vehicle is spotlessly clean inside and purrs away down the street. "So when do you ride your motorcycles if you can't ride them at work?"

He shoots me a look before he goes back to driving. "You caught me out in one of my secrets. I actually don't own a motorcycle of my own."

"Not even one?!" I counter. "I thought you might have a whole warehouse full of them."

He laughs. "I don't need one. I get to ride every kind of motorcycle known to man in my line of work. I get to change motorcycles multiple times a week. I could never own that many motorcycles and I don't even need to. I have all those motorcycles at my fingertips. I get to enjoy them and move on to the next one without the problem of housing them, maintaining them, registering them, and tuning them."

"I never thought of that! That's really cool."

"It's one of the perks of my job. Someone is always bringing in some high-powered crotch-rocket and all the guys take it for a spin. We all stand around oohing and aahing over it, talking about it for hours, and creaming our jeans over it."

I burst out laughing. "I can just imagine! Crotch-rocket! That's hilarious."

"That happens all the time. We all get a thrill over the bike and then the same thing happens a few days later when someone brings in the next one. It's like crack."

I can't stop beaming at him from the side. "You little junkie, you."

"Absolutely." He pulls into the parking lot and lets me out of the passenger door.

We enter a crummy little diner where we're the only customers. We sit down at a table and he orders a full dinner of breaded steak cutlets smothered in gravy, mashed potatoes, and a side salad.

I get a piece of peach pie. I'm not hungry for anything else.

The waitress leaves and Reese extends his hand across the table to take mine. "I'm really sorry about your brother."

I try to shrug it away. "I guess you were right. It's all the other stuff going on in my life that I have to adjust to. His death is kinda far down there on the list right now."

"How are you feeling about the divorce? I understand if you don't want to start up with something else right away."

"Will you stop saying that? We already did start up. Did you really think I could just dump you after everything that happened? You're......"

I break off. I find it hard to look at him, but when I lower my eyes, I wind up looking at our hands joined on the table.

"I'm what?" he asks. "Help me understand what I am in your life. I really need to know."

"You're.....you're the only person who really knows me. What happened on the ship.....it changed my whole life. No one in my family knows about me and Landon. My parents still think I'm going to work it out with him. I just told them yesterday that I moved into the apartment. That's the first they've heard about any problems I had with Landon. They don't know he cheated—and they'll probably never find out everything that happened on the ship. You're the only person who knows. You're the only person I trust."

He squeezes my hand. "I feel the same way about you. I couldn't walk away. I had to come. My life is nothing without you."

I try to make a face, but I wind up wincing instead. "Your life is everything. You have so much going for you. You have this side business you're running and everything. I really admire that about you."

"You have so much going for you, too. You have your whole life in front of you. I don't want to face any of that without you. I need you."

I look up into his eyes and see the same emotion pouring out of him.

I need him, too. I know that now. I can't go back to being alone.

"These last few days....in the apartment...."

"What's wrong with the apartment?" he asks. "I thought you liked it there."

"I do! I love it! It....it feels kind of like the suite on the ship. The apartment has the same style of modern décor. It has the same relaxing feel....except that you weren't there. I kept thinking I was back on the ship......except that you weren't there. Sometimes I think you're just downstairs or working on your business and, in a few minutes, you'll come back and we'll be together again....."

I choke as tears sting my eyes and my throat constricts. I clamp my eyes shut trying to hold back a tide of anguish and longing.

I love the apartment. I never let myself think before right now how much I needed him there—how much I longed for the life we had on the ship.

He squeezes my hand and leans across the table to murmur into my face. "I'm right here, baby. I'm here. As soon as we leave here, I'll take you home and then I will be there. We'll be together again exactly the way we were on the ship. Nothing will change. I love you as much as ever and I know you love me. Nothing can break us apart. I'm here and I'm not going anywhere as long as you want me here."

"I do!" I croak.

"Then you'll never get rid of me. Don't worry. I have to go to work tomorrow, too. You'll have all day by yourself in the apartment. I'll come home in the evening and we'll spend time together then. We'll build a life that works for us. We've already gone through the worst we can possibly go through. We can face anything life throws at us."

I struggle to hold back emotion, and right then, the waitress comes with our food.

Reese squeezes my hand one last time and we pull apart so she can put the food in front of us.

We both thank her and he starts eating. I find it hard to look at Reese sitting across from me.

This is the last thing I ever expected to happen. I never thought I would ever be sitting across the table from him talking about this.

I never thought I would ever hear him say that he would come home with me and we would be together.

I'm not sure if I can handle this. It's more than I can handle.

Chapter 27: Reese

I adjust the knot on my tie to make sure it's straight. Then I check my hair one more time before I pick up my jacket.

Selena comes up behind me and slips her hands around my waist from behind. She nuzzles into my back.

I have to smile when I think about spending the night with her last night. She's as sweet as ever. This apartment really is a real-world copy of our suite on the ship. Everything is the same between us as long as we're here.

I squirm around in her arms so I can kiss her. "How long do you have to stay downtown?"

"I just have to meet with my manager at the agency. I should be home in an hour."

"I'll see you tonight, then. I'll call you at lunchtime, okay?"

"Okay." She gives me one more kiss and breaks away. "I gotta go. Have a good day, okay?"

"I will. I love you."

She blows me a kiss and walks out of the apartment. I don't have to leave for another twenty minutes. That gives me time to check my emails and do a few other things.

I plan to leave early anyway so I can stop by my other hotel room and pick up my stuff. I'll probably be staying here for a while—at least, I hope I will be.

I should talk to Selena about that. I don't want to assume anything. She might want us to live apart for a while.

I'm cool with that. I'm cool with taking things as slow as she needs to. I'm even cool with waiting until her divorce goes through.

I'm just putting my car keys and phone in my pockets to leave when someone knocks on the apartment door. I don't know who it might be, so I answer it.

The woman outside has shoulder-length brown hair, sharp features, and very hard blue eyes. She wears yoga pants and a puffy down vest over a tight long-sleeved T-shirt.

She narrows her eyes at me and her mouth goes hard. "Who the hell are you?" she demands.

"I'm Reese Shipley. Who are you?"

"What the hell are you doing here?"

I frown at her. "What the hell are *you* doing here? Do I know you?"

She glares at me in outright hatred. "This is my sister's apartment. What are you doing in here? Where is she?"

"She just went to work." I hold out my hand to her. "It's nice to meet you. I met your sister on the Paradise Cruise. She told me a lot about you. You're Annabeth, aren't you?"

Her jaw drops and she gasps. "I better not find out you did anything to her!"

"Did anything to her? I'm staying here with her."

She gawks at me in horror like I'm some kind of axe murderer or something. Then she clenches her lips shut again. "Did you break in here after she left? Are you some kind of burglar or something?"

"I just told you. I stayed with your sister on the cruise. I just came to town to see her."

My mind goes into a series of gymnastics when I remember. Selena hasn't told her family about me. She hasn't even told her family about Landon. They don't know anything about her life after she went on the cruise.

They don't even know he cheated on her. They don't know why she moved out of his house.

Annabeth narrows her eyes at me and points in my face. "You stay right where you are, Mister. I'm calling the Police."

"Hey!" I tell her. "I'm not a burglar!"

She ignores me and pulls out her phone. I pull out mine and call Selena. This situation is rapidly disintegrating into a nightmare.

The phone rings and rings and rings. Selena must still be driving. She might even turn off her phone during her meeting with her manager. What if I can't get in touch with her to straighten this out?

Annabeth gets off the phone, plants herself in front of me, and glares at me some more. "You aren't going anywhere, buddy. The Police are on their way."

"I wasn't going anywhere, Annabeth. I wasn't doing anything wrong. Your sister invited me in here to stay. She just left for work."

"I don't know who the hell you think you are, but I swear to God, if I find out you did anything to her, I'll hunt you down and cut you into small pieces." She snarls through gritted teeth. "I swear no one will ever find your body."

"No one did anything to your sister, Annabeth. She went downtown to meet with her manager at the agency. Why don't you call her and find out?"

I barely get the words out before I remember. Annabeth won't be able to call Selena, either. Selena is driving or has her phone turned off.

I decide not to say anything else until the cops show up. They at least have the brains to make Annabeth back off while they interview me.

I give them the same explanation, but they can't get in touch with Selena, either.

"I think you better come down to the station until we can straighten all of this out," one of them tells me.

"Do I have to? I'm supposed to go to work in a few minutes."

"I think this is a little more important, don't you?"

I guess I can't argue with that. They escort me outside. Annabeth glares at me when the cops sit me in the back of their squad car and drive away. At least they don't handcuff me. That would be terrible.

Chapter 28: Selena

I get home from my meeting and sit down at the table to start work when my phone rings. It's Reese. That's strange. He should be in the middle of work right now.

I answer it. "Hey! What's up? It isn't lunchtime, you know."

"I have a problem, baby. I need your help."

"Okay. What's going on?"

"I was getting ready to leave for work this morning—right after you left—and your sister showed up to see you. She got all hostile because she didn't know who I was. She didn't believe me when I told her. She assumed I was either breaking into your apartment or that I did something to you. She called the Police....so I'm at the station right now."

I groan and cover my eyes. "Oh, my God! I can't believe it!"

"The officers have been trying to contact you all morning. I need you to come down here, show them that you're alive and well, and explain to them that you really did invite me into your apartment. They won't let me leave until they hear it from you."

"Okay. I'm on my way. I'm really sorry about all of this."

"Don't apologize for something you didn't do. Just get me the hell out of here. That's all I ask."

"Okay. Sit tight. I'm on my way."

I hang up and race out of the apartment. This disaster is going to go down in the record books. I'm going to have to have a serious conversation with Annabeth—and with the rest of my family.

I didn't plan to jump right into the deep end with Reese, but it looks like I have to.

I burn rubber to the Police station and spent more than an hour explaining everything to the officers. Thank the stars Reese isn't under arrest.

He keeps his guard up until we get outside. "I'm so sorry about this," I tell him. "I feel awful."

"What do you want to do about this?" he asks.

I shuffle my feet. "I think maybe the best thing to do is to introduce you to my family and explain everything that's been going on between us. That's the only way they're going to understand."

He nods, but he has a hard time looking at me. "Okay. It isn't the way I planned for it to happen, but I guess it has to be that way."

"It isn't the way I planned for it to happen, either, but I didn't plan for you to get hauled in by the Police, either. I don't want anything like this to happen again."

"Neither do I."

I lead him to my car and he gets into the passenger seat. We don't talk all the way back to the apartment.

"I'm sorry you missed work today," I tell him.

"It's fine. I already spoke to everyone at the office about it. I had a lot of time sitting around at the Police station, so I did a lot of work on my phone." He looks up at me from the side. "I'm sorry you missed work, too."

"It's okay. It's one of the benefits of keeping my own schedule."

I park outside the building and we go into the apartment. We've only been gone for a few hours. All my work supplies lie out on the table waiting for me.

He throws his phone and car keys on the kitchen counter. I don't blame him for stewing in resentment about this. I would if this happened to me.

I turn around and take a deep breath. "I think....I think you should move in here," I tell him.

His head snaps up and he stares at me with burning intensity. "Are you sure about that?"

"Yes. Absolutely. I think you should make this your permanent address—and put your name on the rental agreement and everything. Today wouldn't have happened if you did that. You could just contact the building manager and he could show the Police that you live here as a tenant."

He stares at me so hard that I think I may have offended him. When he does break eye contact, he unbuttons his jacket, sweeps it aside, sits down on the couch, crosses his legs, and locks his unwavering gaze on me again.

"You just used the word, 'permanent' in relation to us," he begins. "Are you saying what I think you're saying?"

I turn bright red. "I only meant...." I trail off. I don't know what I meant.

"Did you know that these apartments are also for sale?" he asks. "People can buy these apartments and live here permanently. Did you know that?"

Now it's my head that snaps up. "Really? I didn't know."

"Because....if you're serious about us moving in together, we would need a permanent situation—or at least a long-term situation—which this rental isn't. We should think about buying something."

I open my mouth, but no sound comes out. This conversation sure escalated fast.

"You said before that you aren't sure if you'll get enough from the divorce to buy your own place."

"I don't know what I'll get or if I have the credit to buy somethin g....but that was when I was thinking about a house. I never thought about.....*this.*"

I look around the apartment again. I really love this apartment. I especially love what it means to Reese and me. I don't want to give that up.

He pulls out his phone and taps on it. "These apartments go for about a third of what a regular house would cost. I have enough to buy a house—a big house—but I don't want to pressure you into something you aren't ready for. You seem settled here. You seem like you want to stay here for a while."

I can barely make myself heard when I half-whisper, "I do."

"Then I think we should buy this place—jointly. Both of our names would be on the title and we could share the payments fifty-fifty until we're ready to scale up to something bigger. How does that sound?"

I can only nod. He's right. This is more than I'm ready for, but I guess we're doing it.

He holds out his hand and lowers his voice to a husky murmur. "Come here, baby."

I go over there and he steers me down on his lap. I wrap my arms around his neck and rest my head on his shoulder while he holds me.

"I just....I just want to keep going like this," I whisper. "I don't want anything to get in the way."

"That's what I want, too, baby," he murmurs. "I don't want it to ever end."

"I'm so sorry about today. I should have told them before...."

"When would you have told them? You couldn't tell them while you were dealing with your brother's death. Neither of us knew this was going to happen. You didn't even know I was in town until yesterday. You had no reason to tell them."

"I just feel terrible. They think I'm still working things out with Landon and now you and I are talking about moving in together. It isn't fair to you that you and I can be getting so serious and they treat you like an intruder in my life. They don't know who or what you really are. I don't like it at all."

"You'll change it. You'll explain it to them and I'll meet them. We can't expect things to change overnight. So many things have been happening lately. It's hard even for me to keep up with them all. Of course they don't know about me. How could they when you haven't told them?"

I shut my eyes. "I just want us to be together. I wish it didn't have to be so complicated."

"We aren't complicated. We're simple. It's everything else in the world that's complicated. That's the way it's supposed to be. You and I are supposed to be solid against everything the world throws at us."

I sit up to look deep into his eyes. "We are solid. We'll always be solid."

He cups my cheeks and pulls me in to kiss me. We spent last night together, but we didn't have time to really show our passion for each other.

Today going off the rails might be a blessing in disguise. He kisses deeper and hotter by the second. Sitting on his lap turns me on so much.

All the ravenous desire we experienced on the ship comes raging back in an instant. He starts to get hard under me.

I screw my hips down on top of him to make both of us even hotter. He slips his hand between my legs and rubs me until I moan.

I'm just about to turn around and ride him on the couch when he stands up, scoops me up into his arms, and carries me to the bedroom.

I scream when he throws me on the bed and starts yanking his jacket off. "You asked for it. Be grateful I didn't drag you in here by the hair."

I want to make a joke out of that, but I can't do that when I see him unbuttoning his shirt and unbuckling his belt.

My body bursts into flames. I want him like this—all raving wild and determined to get what he wants.

I start scrambling to pull my clothes off fast enough to meet him. I strip naked and sprawl on the bed while he crawls on top of me and sinks down to kiss me.

Our bodies meet in an explosive convulsion of screaming passion. We tumble here, there, and everywhere experiencing everything we had on the ship and so much more.

We finally lie exhausted and sweaty in each other's arms. I sink into his chest and shut my eyes listening to his heart pounding against my ear.

"I should probably go into work for the second half of the day," he murmurs. "It isn't even noon."

"Tell your boss you got arrested."

He snorts. "No. Just no."

I laugh and lean back. "Hey, it was worth it so we could have sex."

"No, it wasn't. What are you going to do about Annabeth?"

My smile evaporates. "Actually I was going to see her as soon as you leave."

"Don't rip her eyes out, okay?"

"I wasn't going to."

"What are you going to do?"

I look up at the ceiling. "Maybe I shouldn't do anything. Maybe I should just email the whole family about what happened. Then they'll know the situation before you meet them."

"That seems to make more sense than you confronting Annabeth about something she knew nothing about."

I spin around. "You're being awfully understanding toward her. I thought you would be more hostile."

"She's being hostile enough for all of us, don't you think? Anyway, your family all thinks you and Landon are just taking a break to work some stuff out. She couldn't possibly know who I am or why I was in your apartment."

"She should have listened to you. She should at least have considered the possibility that you were telling the truth."

"I see it more as she was defending your honor. She probably didn't think it was possible that you could shack up with another guy while you were married to Landon. She probably thinks the only other explanation is that you were the one who cheated and got yourself another guy while he's the injured party."

I blink at him. "I never thought of that."

"See it from her point of view. Her behavior isn't all that out of the ordinary if you think about it."

I lean in and kiss him. "You're so much smarter than I am."

He sits up. "I better go be a responsible adult. Send them an email about what happened so they all understand. Okay? Clear the air."

"Okay. I will."

Chapter 29: Reese

I park my Hummer in front of a quaint little suburban house a few miles from the apartment I now share with Selena. We're preparing to buy it so we can both live there long-term.

I eye the house through the windshield and so does she.

"Annabeth better not pull anything in there," she mutters. "I might have to give her a smackdown."

"Don't go in expecting that. Just plan on explaining everything to them."

I make a face, but I don't argue. I already sent my parents, Annabeth, and everyone else who is going to be here a lengthy email about Reese and everything leading up to how we came to be moving in together.

Everyone here knows as much as I do, but I still brace myself for the worst.

Reese lets me out of the passenger seat, takes my hand, and murmurs, "Here goes nothing."

We head up the garden walk to the front door. I walk in without knocking. I never have to knock to enter my parents' house.

I find my mom and dad in the kitchen. I hug and kiss them both and introduce them to Reese.

They shake his hand, smile, and welcome him. They both tell him it's a pleasure to meet him, but I can't help feeling the nervous tension in the air. They're being formally polite. That's all.

I lead him into the living room. Annabeth is in there with her husband, Jimmy. The patio doors stand open to the deck where Jimmy's brother Allen and Allen's wife Kelly work on the barbecue.

Annabeth is busy straightening the clothes of one of Allen's and Kelly's children. Little Rex is only two. I don't see what's wrong with his clothes. She doesn't look up when I walk in with Reese.

Jimmy shakes hands with Reese when I introduce them. Jimmy is also welcoming and polite. He's much more relaxed about it than my parents were.

Annabeth straightens up, gives Reese one look, and walks out onto the deck where she starts doing anything and everything other than talking to him.

I try to ignore her, but my hackles already start to rise. She better not turn this into an awkward nightmare. I really will have to smack her down if she does.

Jimmy takes Reese under his wing right away, waves him outside, and takes over the introductions. Allen and Kelly also shake hands, smile, and tell Reese it's nice to meet him.

Jimmy gives Reese a bottle of beer to drink. The four of them stand around the barbecue talking.

It takes them about ten seconds to find out what Reese does for a living. Then the whole conversation devolves into an enormous block party talking about motorcycles and gushing about this or that model.

Allen and Kelly are huge motorcycle people—or they were before they started having kids. They used to go touring around the country in massive convoys with other riders.

They got my brother Anderson into it, too, and they've been trying to get Jimmy and Annabeth involved for years. Jimmy wants to. Annabeth doesn't. She thinks it's a waste of time.

She doesn't come over. She busies herself fussing over Allen's and Kelly's kids. They're just fine playing in the backyard. They don't need anyone fussing over them. She's only doing it to avoid Reese.

I join him and the others even though I don't know enough about motorcycles to participate in the conversation. I love watching him work the room—or the yard as the case happens to be.

He holds the other three in the palm of his hand, tells them fascinating stories tells them jokes to make them laugh, and astounds them all by telling them about his website business and forum.

They all want to join it. He gives them the link and they give him their email addresses. He really is a master of his craft.

My dad comes over while they are talking. He joins our circle, but he doesn't know enough about motorcycles to participate, either.

He definitely appreciates Reese's wit and banter. My dad laughs at Reese's jokes and listens to his stories. Everyone here is having a good time.

Annabeth uses some excuse to walk past us and goes inside to help my mom in the kitchen. Allen keeps breaking away from the conversation to turn things over on the barbecue and add new things to it.

A few minutes later, Annabeth comes out to call Jimmy inside. One of Kelly's kids starts crying and she leaves to deal with the situation.

I touch Reese on the elbow. "I'm going to help my mom set the table. Are you okay out here for now?"

"Yeah, I'm fine," he replies. "See you later."

I leave him with Allen and my dad. Reese will be fine with them. I know he'll be fine in general now.

My mom, Annabeth, and I set the buffet table in the living room. Annabeth takes the plates and glasses while I take the silverware.

I'm just on my way back to the kitchen when I notice something out of place. Annabeth comes back just then carrying a crockpot full of my mom's baked beans.

"You deliberately put out the wrong number of plates and glasses," I tell her. "You left one out to make a point about Reese. Didn't you?"

She snaps, "I don't know what you're talking about," and turns away.

I grab her arm to hold her back. "You better drop the hostility real quick. You have no right to hold it against him when you were the one who made a mistake about him being in my apartment."

"I didn't make a mistake about you cheating on your husband so you could hook up with a total stranger," she fires back. "I really thought you were better than that, Selena."

"He was the one who cheated on me!" I counter. "I told you what happened in the email. I can understand you wanting to protect me when you found Reese alone in my apartment, but you know the situation now. You better drop this and start getting along with him."

"I don't have to do anything," she snaps. "You go sleep around with him if you want to. You won't get me to approve of anything."

"I'm not sleeping around with anyone, Annabeth! Reese and I have been together for weeks! You just didn't know about it. Now you do, so clean up your attitude."

My mom comes in just then to put a pan of cornbread on the table. Like magic, Allen, Reese, and my dad all come in from outside at the same time.

Jimmy comes down the hall from the bathroom. Kelly walks into the living room carrying Rex.

Everyone hears the last of my confrontation with Annabeth. Now everyone is in the same room. It's the perfect storm.

"We aren't here to sit in judgment of Reese or Selena," my dad begins. "What they do is none of our business."

"It was pretty obvious who did what from that email," Jimmy adds. "I'm really sorry you had to go through all that, Selena. It sounds terrible."

"How can you defend her?" Annabeth snaps. "There are two sides to every story. I'm sure Landon has a completely different version of events."

"I'm your sister, Annabeth!" I counter. "You would rather take Landon's side than mine?!"

"No one made Landon get thrown off the cruise ship for drunken disorderly conduct and aggravated assault," Reese chimes in. "That's Landon's side of the story."

I pull out my phone and shove it in Annabeth's face. "Do you see that? Do you see that?! That's a picture I took of him making out with a woman from his office in the middle of the workday! This is right outside the hospital where I was putting Ashton's car seat in my car. Do you remember that? This is how I found out what Landon was doing. He cheated on me with three other women before I broke up with him—and I broke up with him before I ever got together with Reese."

"When you broke up with him and when you got together with Reese aren't our business, either, sweetheart," my dad tells me. "You're a part of this family. Landon isn't. Whoever you spend your time with is welcome here no matter who it is."

"Speak for yourself," Annabeth snaps. "If I find out you did wrong by Landon....."

"You'll do what?" I counter. "What could you possibly do? You won't speak to me again? I really hope you don't after what you did."

"What did she do?" Kelly asks.

"Reese got arrested, okay?" Annabeth blurts out. "He got arrested and dragged off to the Police station in the back of a squad car! That's the kind of person we're letting into our family. Are you happy now?"

"Are you sure about this, sweetheart?" my mom interjects. "Why can't you and Landon work this out somehow? Why throw away a good thing?"

"You didn't read the email," my dad tells her. "Don't talk about how good their marriage was until you read it."

"Reese did not get arrested!" I snap. "Annabeth is lying to smear him in front of all of you and make you think he's a bad person when she was the one who screwed up. She showed up unannounced when I wasn't there and she was the one who jumped to conclusions when she found Reese there alone. She refused to listen to his explanation about what he was doing there and she called the Police on him. She didn't even bother to confirm it first. I can't believe you, Annabeth. I can't believe you would be so vindictive as to bring that up now just to turn the family against him."

"I agree with Selena," Jimmy adds. "You owe Reese an apology, Annabeth."

She rounds on her husband. "How dare you take their side? I'm your wife!"

"That's exactly why I'm saying it. You should have apologized and made up with Reese and Selena the minute you read her email. You know you made a mistake. Just own up."

Annabeth throws up her hands and spins away. "I'm not going to listen to this from my own husband!"

She storms out through the patio doors and vanishes into the backyard.

"I think I better leave," Reese murmurs. "I didn't mean to cause so much trouble."

"You don't have to go, son," my dad tells him. "We really would like you to stay."

Reese murmurs, "I don't think so. Thanks for your hospitality," and walks out of the house.

"Maybe we should all sit down and talk about this," my mom quavers.

"You aren't going to talk about anything until you read that email," my dad tells her.

"I better go, too." I kiss my dad on the cheek. "Thank you, Dad. I'll see you later."

"Don't leave, Selena!" Jimmy exclaims. "We can talk some sense into Annabeth."

"You do that. I need to take care of Reese right now."

I storm out of the house just as Reese is starting the motor on the Hummer. He really would have driven off alone. I don't blame him.

I get into the passenger seat, slam the door, and he drives off.

Chapter 30:
Reese

I kick my feet up on the living room coffee table and prop my laptop on my thighs. I'm just getting comfortable when someone knocks on the apartment door. I'm really starting to hate that sound.

I dread what I'll find when I open it, but I have to meet the enemy head on.

I open the door and freeze when I see Selena's father Walter standing there. "Um...hello....." I greet him. "Can I help you with something? Selena isn't here. She had to go meet someone at the agency."

He grins at me. "I know that. How you doing, son?"

"Um....I'm fine. To what do I owe the pleasure?"

"I thought I would drop by and see if you want to go out for a while."

I raise my eyebrows. "Out? What do you mean by out?"

"We could play golf—shoot some pool—have lunch. I know you're into motorcycles, but I have never ridden one, so I'm sorry to say we couldn't do that. But I thought I would just see if you want to hang out and spend some time together—just to get to know each other—just you and me—apart from Selena and the rest of the family. What do you say? Do you play golf?"

"Uh....yeah. I play it, but I'm not very good."

He laughs. "Neither am I. Come on. Let's get out of here—unless you're in the middle of something important."

"I'm not. Today's my day off."

He grins at me again. "I know. I checked. I wanted to make sure you had some time off when Selena wasn't around—so we could talk man to man."

"So.....this is the father-in-law talk. Is that it?"

"No, no! Nothing like that. This is just a casual hang-out-and-shoot-the-breeze thing."

"Uh.....okay. Why aren't we having the father-in-law talk?"

"Because I already approve of you, son. Selena was very specific in her email about everything that happened between you two on the cruise ship—*everything* that happened. You have nothing to worry about. I know you're a good man and I know you would do anything necessary to take care of my daughter."

"Of course I would. I love her. I moved across the country just to be with her."

"Exactly." He waves behind him. "Are you coming?"

I have no reason not to, so I gather my phone, keys, and wallet and follow him outside.

He opens the passenger door of a beautiful white Lincoln Zephyr. It's one of the nicest cars I've ever seen.

He grins at me and sets off driving through town. I feel a little awkward about going out with him after the disaster at his house.

"You don't have your own golf clubs, do you?" he asks on the way. "I should have asked before we left your place, but I figured you might not after you said you weren't any good."

"I don't have my own clubs. I usually just rent a set from whatever course I'm playing on."

"I do the same thing. I figure what's the point in buying my own clubs? Maybe I'll buy myself a nice set when I get good enough to compete on the PGA tour."

He laughs at his own joke. I find myself squirming. I've never met a woman's father before. I never thought it would go like this.

"So what do you like to do apart from ride motorcycles?" he asks.

"I like scuba diving and birdwatching. Selena and I plan to take trips together so we can do it in different parts of the world."

"That's great! She was really into scuba before she got together with Landon. She got certified and everything."

I have to ask. "Did you approve of Landon?"

"I never disapproved of him. He was young when they got together. He never distinguished himself—not the way you did—but then again, he never really had a chance to." He glances over at me. "What you did on the ship—that kind of thing takes maturity. It sounds like he never really developed it."

I look out the window. I don't want to talk about what I did on the ship. I don't see how I could have done anything else.

"I feel bad," I mumble. "I feel responsible for Selena getting hurt. She never would have gotten hurt if I hadn't brought Zaria into the picture."

"You couldn't know your girlfriend would fly off the handle like that. The important thing is that you handled it. That's all you can do in situations like that. Anyway, you're the one who saved Selena from that. I'm grateful."

He pulls into the parking lot at the golf course. It's a big, manicured, sprawling course with some expensive limos and sports cars in the parking lot.

I point at one of the sports cars when we get out. "I know that guy. He's one of my new clients."

Walter brightens up. "It's awesome that you can talk to so many people so effortlessly about what you love."

"Sure. Talking about motorcycles is easy. Everybody loves them."

He laughs and we go inside. He has a membership here, so maybe he was pulling my leg about not being very good at the game.

He pays for both of us to rent clubs, balls, and golf cart. I'm not sure I like where this is going.

Some of my new clients, customers, and retailers come up to me in the lobby. Walter stands off to one side while I shake hands and joke around with them.

They ask me what I'm doing there and I mention that I'm here with Walter. They all know him, too, and the conversation shifts.

It comes out that I'm dating his daughter, Selena, and that I moved here to be with her after I met her on a cruise ship. He laughs when they give me a hard time about it.

We finally break away and drive out onto the course. He will not stop grinning at me. "You're an asset, son."

"Hardly," I mutter.

We get out at the first hole and tee up. We both swing and drive our balls down the links. Then we drive to the putting green.

I wait and lean on my club while he lines up his putt. "Don't worry about the family," he tells me over his shoulder. "I'm sure all of this will blow over."

"It will blow over when Jimmy and Annabeth get a divorce," I grumble. "Then Annabeth will still be in the family and I'll be down another ally."

He laughs. "They won't get divorced. Annabeth will come around. You'll see."

"What makes you so sure?"

He sinks his putt and stands up to beam at me. "I know my daughters too well. She'll pull her head in and the whole family will accept you. Take my word for it. I know them better than you do."

I find myself eyeing him. "Are you saying that because you'll have something to do with it?"

He laughs. "I never said that."

"Why are you doing this?" I ask. "You don't know me from a hole in the ground."

"A father always wants what's best for his children. I've been around long enough to know it when I see it." He pats me on the shoulder. "Take your putt and live to rue the day."

Now it's my turn to laugh. He sure is friendly and warm. I really hope it stays that way.

Chapter 31: Reese

Walter dunks his French fry into a puddle of ketchup on his plate, raises it like he's making a toast, and smirks at me when he sticks it in his mouth. "Today was a great day, son. We should do it more often."

"What are you going to do about Annabeth—and anyone else who might want to aim a pitchfork at my head?"

He laughs again. He laughs a lot. "You're funny! I can see why Selena likes you—I mean apart from all the other stuff."

"Well? I feel like I need to wear a Kevlar vest the next time I come over to your place."

"You don't need to do that. In fact, you don't need to do anything—about any of it."

"You're going to have to do better than that if you expect me to believe that."

"What I mean is....you don't have to do anything about it because I already did."

I raise my eyebrows. "What did you do?"

"I had a quiet word with a few key people, including Annabeth and her mother. I didn't have to have a quiet word with Jimmy and Allen because they already think you're the greatest thing since sliced bread."

"They're going to be awfully disappointed when they find out I'm not."

He laughs again. "What I mean is I didn't have to have a word with them about you. I had a word with them about Annabeth and Kelly. I can't be certain, but I'm pretty sure Kelly thinks you're something special after the way you were talking to her and Allen about motorcycles, but I had a word with him anyway."

"About what?"

"About both of them keeping their wives in line. Jimmy was already Team Reese, let me tell you."

I snort. "So now we're picking teams?"

"What I mean is that I already gave her the hard word to get in line and read the writing on the wall—or more to the point, to read the writing in the email. I'm not sure if she even read the email, but I told her to either read it and fully understand what it said or to re-read it and fully understand what it said because I wasn't going to stand her saying and doing something against someone who was so obviously protective and caring toward Selena if you know what I mean."

I look away. "I feel awful that I brought this kind of turmoil to your family. It isn't what I intended at all."

"You didn't. Don't you see? You didn't at all. You saved my daughter's life. If you don't belong in the family, I don't know who does. That's a hell of a lot more than I can say for Jimmy—or anyone else. Hell, even I haven't saved my wife's life."

I don't like him talking about me like that. "How do you know Annabeth will get in line?"

"Oh, she will. Trust me."

"I just don't want to go through another family get-together like the last one."

"You won't. I give you my word of honor as a father, a husband, and a man. The next time you set foot in my house—or in any other house belonging to anyone who was there, you will be welcomed and honored the way you deserve."

"I don't think I deserve to be honored for doing the right thing."

"Call it what you want." He wipes his mouth, wads up his napkin, and tosses it on his plate. "Are you ready to go?"

"Yeah. I've been ready to go for half an hour. I've just been sitting here watching you eat."

He laughs again. "Don't tell my wife."

He slides out of the booth, goes to the counter to pay the check, and we leave the hamburger joint downtown. We've been here ever since we finished our golf game.

We get in his car and drive back to the apartment complex. He walks me up to the door of the building.

"I meant what I said," he tells me. "I don't want you to feel any hesitation about coming over—to any of our houses. You'll be welcome as long as you and Selena are together."

"Thank you. I really appreciate your intervention—and for today. I had a really good time."

He grins and pats me on the arm. "And don't worry too much that you don't believe me or trust me or maybe you don't even like me."

"I do. I just....I've never dated a girl whose father did something like this."

He laughs. "I'm glad I could be the first. Have a great rest of your day off. I'm sure I'll see you around."

He's just getting ready to go back to his car when Selena pulls in and parks. Her eyes bug out when she sees us together through the windshield.

Walter grins at me. "Uh-oh. We're busted."

"Were we doing something wrong?" I ask.

He laughs again.

She gets out of her car, stares at us, and then walks over. "Dad?" She glances at me. "What's going on?"

"Nothing is going on, sweetheart." He kisses her on the cheek. "I just took Reese out for lunch and a game of golf. We talked. That's all you need to know." He smiles at me. "See you later, buddy."

He walks back to his car. Selena stares up at me. "What the hell just happened?"

"He took me out to lunch—and a game of golf."

"Is that all?" She narrows her eyes. "It seems like there should be more to the story than that."

"He says he had a few words with Annabeth and the others—and your mother. He says he straightened the whole thing out."

Her jaw drops. "He did?"

I nod. "He's something else, I tell you what."

She gapes at me for a second, and before I can think twice, she spins away, charges across the parking lot, and tackles him in a huge hug.

She practically topples him against the car, yelling, "I love you, Dad!!" She kisses him on the cheek.

He laughs again, pats her on the back, and says, "I love you, too, sweetheart. You better go inside. I'll see you soon."

She backs off and he gets into his car. He waves to both of us with a big smile on his face when he starts the motor and drives away.

She backs away and comes toward me. "Is there something else I should know about this?"

"No." I turn away and lead her inside. "He just said he approves of me and he wants me to feel welcome whenever I come over. He says he wants to make sure Annabeth and everyone else understand that I'm.....well, I guess he meant that he thinks I'm good for you."

She slips her hand into mine. "You are good for me."

I can't help but smile at her. "You're good for me, too. He was really great. I had a great time and he says he wants to do it more often."

"Wow. That's big."

"Did he do that with Landon?"

"No, nothing like that. My parents were always kind of neutral on Landon—but then again, he was always kind of neutral in general."

"That's what your dad said."

"What else did he say?"

I shrug that away. I don't want to repeat what he said. "That's about it. He doesn't think Annabeth read your email, or if she did, she didn't fully understand it."

"I guess that makes sense considering the way she acted."

"I think maybe she might have been embarrassed about the way she reacted when she met me here. Maybe she felt like she had to defend herself."

"You're much more forgiving than I would be—and you're the one she insulted."

"I don't feel insulted. I just want it to work out between me and your family—just like I want it to work out between me and you."

She beams at me. "I want it to work out, too."

I pull her down next to me on the couch and put my keys and phone on the table in front of me so they don't take up so much room in my pocket.

"Sit down, baby. I want to talk to you about something."

"Okay. What is it?"

"It's about....us....about what we both said about it working out between us."

"Yeah. We both want it to."

"That's what I want to talk about."

"What's wrong with both of us wanting it to work out?"

"The part about wanting it to. If we both want it to, then there's only one more step to take and that's to make it work out between us."

She frowns. "I don't understand. What do you mean."

"I mean.....we would commit to each other and say we're going to make it work no matter what. We aren't going to *want* it to work out. We're *going* to make it work because we're going to stay together no matter what."

Her eyes widen. "Commit."

"Yes. We're living together. We're buying this apartment together. We both want it to work. What's stopping us."

She opens her mouth, but right then, my phone rings on the table in front of me. I don't intend to pick it up, but I can't help but see the screen from here. The call is from my brother, Aaron.

I pick up the phone while I try to decide whether to take it. "Answer it," Selena tells me.

I answer it. "Yeah."

"Hey, man," he greets me.

"Hey, what's up?"

"I'm in town. I just flew in to see you. I want to meet with you as soon as it's reasonably convenient for you."

I stare at nothing. "You're....you're here? Like....in the same town as me?"

"I'm staying in a hotel downtown. I want to meet you if you aren't doing anything. I'm in the Marriot Four Seasons. I can meet you in the bar downstairs—anytime you say. I'll be staying here until I see you."

"Um.....why are you here? Aren't you supposed to be across the country?"

"I'm here to see you. It's important."

I frown. It must be important if he flew all the way out here to see me. He could have just called or sent me a text.

"Uh....okay, man. I can be there in half an hour."

"Perfect. I'll see you there."

I hang up and stare at my phone.

"What was that about? He's your older brother, isn't he?"

"He flew into town to see me. He's staying in a hotel downtown waiting for me to come talk to him. He says it's important."

"It must be if he came all this way. I hope everyone at home is okay."

"He would have just called if it was that."

"You better go find out what he wants."

I look up at her. "Are you okay with this?"

"Of course. He's family. Bring him over afterward if you want to. I'd like to meet him—or if he wants to. Maybe he wants to fly straight back, but if he wants to, I would love to meet anyone from your family."

I dive in and kiss her on the cheek. "I love you. I'll be back as soon as I can."

Chapter 32: Reese

I skid into the parking lot outside the Marriot Four Seasons Hotel, park my car, and march inside. Whatever my brother Aaron wants, I better get it out on the table.

I head for the bar and he stands up from his table when he sees me coming toward him. I give him a hug and sit down. "You should have told me you were coming into town," I tell him. "I would have picked you up from the airport."

"I didn't want to see you like that. I wanted to sit down so we could talk."

"What about? What's so important?'

He rests his elbows on the table and gets serious. Talking to him is like talking to an older version of myself.

"I'm here on behalf of the whole family. We want to know why you packed up, quit your job, and moved across the country for a woman you don't even know—a woman you met on a cruise. It isn't like you. It isn't responsible—not the way we expect you to be. We need answers. We don't even know this woman. She could be anyone. How do we know she isn't using you and wringing you of every last penny you own?"

I shake my head. "It isn't like that. It's serious."

"How can we trust that? What are we supposed to think? You were going out with Zaria for three years, and the next minute, you go on a cruise, hook up with a total stranger, and throw your whole life away."

"I didn't throw my whole life away—and I didn't quit my job. I just transferred to another office in the same company. I'm still making the same salary and doing the same job."

"Why?" he counters. "You barely came home for more than a day before you left. You must have transferred while you were still on the ship. You must have planned this whole move while you were still on the ship."

I nod. "Yeah. I did."

"And you didn't even tell us—your own family?"

"You don't understand. There were extenuating circumstances."

"Then you're going to have to explain it to me because it looks awfully fishy from where I sit—from where all of us sit. We're worried about you....."

"You don't have to be. You should be happy for me."

He leans back in his seat and raises both hands. "I can't be until I understand."

"First of all, you should know that Zaria was cheating on me with dozens of guys the whole time we were together. It might even have been hundreds of guys."

His eyes fall out of their sockets. "You can't be serious. She worshiped you."

"Maybe, but she just couldn't stop playing the field. She flirted with guys right in front of me. She hooked up with guys in bar bathrooms and back alleys and hallways. She tried to hook up with guys everywhere—and always quick, wham-bam hookups—nothing ongoing. When I finally confronted her and demanded to know exactly how many guys she slept with while we were together, she refused to tell me even if it meant us getting back together—so that tells you it was a lot."

He winces, looks away, and hisses through his teeth. "Jesus! I'm so sorry, man!"

"There's more. I caught her and broke up with her. She came up with the idea of going on the cruise to patch things up. I said it wouldn't and I told her I was going on the cruise to find someone else. She flirted with guys right in front of me on the cruise, too. She even flirted with married male members of the crew and staff."

He won't even look at me. He keeps his eyes down. "I don't need to hear anymore."

"Yes, you do. You said you wanted to understand about me and Selena. Now you're going to hear everything whether you want to or not. I confronted Zaria about hitting on this married guy at the bar. It turns out he was the Chief of Security for the boat. I stormed off and I saw a girl sitting outside crying. I tried to talk to her and it turned out that she was married and had caught her husband cheating four different times. He was the one who wanted her to come on the cruise so they could patch it up and then he proposed to do a couples swap where she hooked up with the guy and he hooked up with the girl. She broke it off with him and she was crying because she realized her marriage was over."

His eyebrows shoot up. "That was her? That was...."

"Selena. I told her we should go through with it to get back at both of them, so we did. Her husband got extremely jealous, but we did it anyway and she and I hit it off immediately. We spent two blissful days together and neither of us wanted it to end. I said we should rent the suite, spend the rest of the cruise together, and never go back to the cheating bastards."

He puffs out his cheeks. "Whoa, man. That is some heavy-duty shit right there."

"Her husband went completely off the rails. He got in my face, got dragged off by security, and then did the same thing again when he was shit-faced drunk and assaulted me right in front of the security guys. He got himself choppered off the ship in handcuffs."

Aaron bursts out in snorting laughter. "I bet he did."

"Zaria also went completely off the rails. First, she had a panic attack when I told her we would never get back together. She got herself sent to the ship's infirmary, stole a deadly drug from the place, and used it to try to poison Selena."

"Oh, my God!" he gasps. "She did not."

"It gets worse. Selena survived, obviously, so Zaria tried to get close to her and actually pushed Selena over the side and into the ocean. She was still weak from the poisoning, so I jumped in and helped her stay afloat until the crew came out to rescue her. The security team got the whole thing on video. They arrested Zaria and called in the chopper to take her off the boat, but she escaped and attacked me and Selena in our suite with a knife. Now she's facing four counts of attempted murder up in New York."

He shakes his head. "Okay. I take it all back. Now I understand."

"The day after the attack, Selena got a phone call that her brother got hit by a car and wasn't expected to make it. She had to fly back here early, but she didn't get here in time. She went through a painful time with her family burying her brother and everything while I was left on the boat alone. I didn't want to keep going without her. I fell in love with her. What I have with her is like nothing I've ever felt. I'm not going back home—not unless something goes catastrophically wrong." I hesitate only a split second before I say what's really on my mind. "I'm going to marry her."

My brother stares at me like he really can't believe I just said those words out loud.

I can't believe I just said those words out loud, but I sure have been thinking them lately. She's the one. She has to be.

We've already gone through the worst. I don't want to lose her. If anything else bad happens, I want us to face it together. What other qualification is there for marriage?

Aaron finally shakes his head and looks away. "Wow, man. That is some story. I still don't like having you living across the country where we can't see each other, but I understand now. Now I just have to explain it to everyone else in the family."

"You don't have to. I'll email everyone and tell them what happened on the cruise. That's what Selena is doing with her family. You can tell everyone that you saw me and heard it from me firsthand. That should be enough. It isn't like I'm out of the family and will never see you again."

"Yeah, I know....."

"Why don't you come back to the apartment and meet her?"

His head shoots up. "Really?"

"Yeah. You'll realize how great she is once you meet her—and she said she wants to meet you if you have time. Come on. Let's go."

He hesitates and then agrees. We stand up, go outside, and I put him in the passenger seat of my car.

We talk about other things on the way back to the apartment. He doesn't mention my story or Selena. He talks about the family.

Then he asks about my job and my web business. He relaxes even more when he hears that I'm keeping up all the same activities I was doing at home.

I start to get nervous when we pull into the parking lot outside the apartment building. This better not turn into a standoff the way it did with Selena's family.

I already know it won't because Aaron knows the story behind me and Selena now. They're both reasonable people and she wants to meet him.

I can't help but get shaky when I unlock the door and walk in. She jumps up from the living room table where she sits working on one of her drawings.

She hustles over to us and bursts into a grin. "Hey! Look who's here! Wow! You look exactly like Reese."

Aaron laughs. "I'm older, so technically he's the one who looks like me." He sticks out his hand. "I'm Aaron Shipley."

"Selena Neise....." She grimaces. "Née Gordon."

He shakes her hand. "Great to meet you. Reese has just been telling me all about your harrowing ordeal on the cruise ship."

She makes another face. "We don't talk about that. Come on in. Make yourself at home. Are you hungry? We haven't had dinner yet. We would love it if you joined us."

"I haven't eaten yet, but I don't want to impose."

"You wouldn't be." She heads for the kitchen. "How about something to drink?"

"I should probably decline that, too. I just had one at the hotel while Reese and I were talking." He stops next to the table and bends over to look at what she's working on. "This is incredible! Did you do this?"

"Oh, that's just one of my illustration contracts. I'm a contract illustrator for children's books. This one is an undersea adventure story for pre-teens."

"It's amazing! You're so talented."

She laughs. "It pays the bills and I love it, so I can't complain, right?"

She comes back, hands me a drink, and makes eye contact with me before she heads over to the couch. I sit down next to her.

I feel like I should be saying something, but they're talking so well that I don't want to interrupt.

"How long are you in town for?" she asks.

He eases over to the living room and sits down in an armchair across from us. "I have a reservation to fly home tomorrow morning, but it's changeable. I didn't know how long I would have to stay or if I would have to carry out some kind of intervention to pry Reese out of your cold, skeletal fingers."

She bursts out laughing and holds up both hands. "My cold, skeletal fingers aren't holding onto anything."

He smiles at her. "I see that. Thank you for being so understanding."

She snorts. "I wish I could get my family to listen to reason the way you are."

"Don't they?"

"Most do. A few of them are a little thicker in the head than others."

"That sucks. I hope they come around—but if they don't, you two are always welcome on our side of the country."

She beams at him. "Thank you. I'll do my best to take good care of your brother."

Aaron looks back and forth between us sitting next to each other on the couch. "It looks like you already are."

Just then, someone knocks on the apartment door. I don't want to break the obvious connection between Aaron and Selena, so I go over there to see who it is.

I open the door and the world stops again when I come face to face with Annabeth. I'm not sure what to say at first.

I stand there staring at her trying to figure it out. Should I act defensive? I don't want to invite her in while Aaron is here. I don't want Annabeth to spoil what's going on between Aaron and Selena. It's too good to let her poison interfere.

She stares back at me like she's going through the same mental struggle. She looks like she can't decide if she wants to be hostile toward me or not.

Actually she looks like she still is hostile toward me and is trying her best not to be for some reason. I wish she wouldn't try. I just want her to be outright hostile instead of trying to hide it—if that is what she's trying to do.

I stand there in silence for so long that Selena comes over to see what the problem is. She goes rigid when she sees her sister.

"What do you want?" Selena snaps.

"I want to talk to you," Annabeth replies in a rush.

"Well, we don't want to talk to you," Selena fires back. "You already said everything you have to say. We don't need to hear it again."

"No, really," Annabeth blurts out. "I really need to talk to you. It's important."

"Not important enough for you to care about your own sister," Selena clips. "Unless you're here to give us an unequivocal, unconditional apology saying what a horrible person you were and how terribly you acted, you can turn around, walk away, get in your car, and drive back to Jimmy or whoever the hell else will put up with your stupid, childish behavior. We have better things to do and better people to spend our time with."

"That's what I'm here for!" Annabeth exclaims. "That's exactly why I'm here."

Selena frowns at her. "What?"

Annabeth opens her mouth, goes through another painful internal commotion, and turns to me. "I'm sorry, Reese! I'm really sorry! I should have listened to you—and I should have read your email, Selena. I screwed up. I know that now. I didn't realize....and I didn't act caring toward you, Selena. I never should have taken Landon's side or assumed anything. I was wrong. I'm ashamed of myself. That's why I'm here. I don't want you to feel uncomfortable about coming to family gatherings or anything."

Selena snorts again. "I don't believe you, Annabeth. I don't believe you're really here apologizing because you feel sorry. Dad told you to come here, didn't he—him and Jimmy? Just admit it. You're here because they put pressure on you to change your attitude."

"No!" Annabeth practically yells. "I mean...they did put pressure on me to change my attitude, but neither of them told me to come here. Neither of them told me to apologize."

"What did they say?" I ask.

"They told me......they both told me to read your email. I didn't before. I'm sorry! I should have. I just thought your email would be a bunch of justifications and excuses and stupid remarks about how Landon wasn't satisfying you or something like that. I had no idea it would be......*that.* You have to believe me—both of you. I'm really sorry. I had no idea about any of what happened on the cruise—or before....."

I look down at Selena. She looks up at me at the same time. I think we should give Annabeth a second chance, but it's really up to Selena. She's Annabeth's sister—and in a way, Annabeth hurt Selena worse than she hurt me.

I see the truth in Selena's eyes, too. She wants to give Annabeth another chance, too. Selena just doesn't want to let Annabeth off the hook so easily.

The three of us are still standing there in silence when Aaron comes up behind us. "Maybe I should get out of here. I don't feel right about being here for this."

Selena whips around fast. "No! Don't leave, Aaron. We were just talking. This is my sister, Annabeth—one of the thick-headed people I was just telling you about. Annabeth, this is Aaron Shipley, Reese's brother."

Aaron holds out his hand to Annabeth. "Nice to meet you."

They shake hands and Annabeth nods. "Nice to meet you, too. You look exactly like your brother."

Aaron smiles. "Everyone says that. You and your sister look nothing alike. I never would have known you were sisters."

Annabeth laughs. "Everyone says that. Selena and Anderson were the ones that looked like twins. No one even knew I was even in the same family."

The tension starts to dissolve. Selena finally waves everyone inside. "You guys might as well sit down. There's no point standing around in the doorway."

We all head back to the living room. Selena and I resume our former positions on the couch. Aaron and Annabeth sit in the armchairs next to each other.

"So what brings you out this far?" Annabeth asks Aaron.

"I came out here to drag my brother away from the vile temptress who kidnapped him off the cruise ship. That was the story I told myself, at least."

She laughs again. "Thank God I'm not the only one who thought that."

"Zaria thought that, too," Selena mutters.

Annabeth's smile evaporates and she spins around to gape at her sister. "Oh, my God! I never realized I was thinking the same way she did!" She covers her face. "Now I really feel like an asshole."

"Just don't do it again and we'll be square."

Annabeth sits up, shakes it off, and turns back to Aaron. "Are you in the motorcycle industry, too?"

"Hell no!" Aaron counters. "Reese is the only freak into all of that."

Annabeth laughs again. "You better not say anything like that around my family. They're all hardcore true believers. I'm the only sane person in the bunch."

"We'll convert you all one day," I interrupt and make everyone laugh.

"He's been trying for years," Aaron tells them.

Selena throws up her hands. "I'm staying out of this one. I'm Switzerland."

"Switzerland can still get invaded, you know," I tell her.

Annabeth holds her hands in front of her face. "Okay! That's my cue to skedaddle." She stands up. "I'll leave you folks alone."

Selena and I walk her to the door. Annabeth turns to me on the threshold. "I'm really sorry about all of this, Reese. Give me a chance and I swear I'll make it up to you."

"Okay," I tell her. "If you can do that, I'll be very happy to put it behind us."

She holds out her hand to me. "Welcome to the family. I realize now that you really are the best man for my sister."

I shake her hand. "Thank you."

She turns to Selena. The two sisters stare at each other and then rush each other in a hug.

Annabeth's voice cracks when she murmurs in Selena's ear. "I love you."

"I love you, too. I'll see you soon."

They separate and Annabeth leaves. Aaron stands up when we turn around. "I should go, too."

"You don't have to!" Selena tells him. "We would love it if you stayed for dinner."

"I don't think so. I think I better head back." He looks at me. "If you don't mind."

"Of course. Let's go."

I kiss Selena and drive him back to the hotel. "You're right," he tells me on the way. "She's really special."

"I told you so."

He claps me on the shoulder. "So when do you plan to propose?"

"Tonight after I drop you off."

He laughs. "You don't wait around, do you? I don't blame you. Go get her and make sure you keep her."

"I will. Don't worry."

He chuckles to himself. "Meeting her only makes me wish even more that you guys lived on our side of the country."

"Maybe we'll move sometime......" Then I remember Walter. "But probably not."

"You'll just have to come visit more often." I pull into the hotel parking lot. He lays his hand on my arm to stop me from turning off the car. "Don't get out."

"Are you sure? I don't like you blowing into town and blowing straight back out again. I want to spend some time with you."

"Go home," he tells me. "Go home to your lady and propose. Don't think about me or the family or anything else."

He gets out of the car, shuts the door, and strides across the parking lot to the lobby. He doesn't look back even once, not even to wave goodbye to me.

I watch him vanish into the building. I'm not sure how to feel about this.

I don't like my brother walking out of my life like this, but another part of me knows he's right.

I plan to propose to Selena the minute I get back to the apartment. I don't want anything to distract me from that.

I have a lot on my mind on the way there. The whole Annabeth situation is settled now—or it seems to be. It remains to be seen if she actually makes good on her promise.

I want to believe her. She says she didn't read the email. I guess that explains why she acted the way she did.

I park outside the apartment building. Aaron sounds awfully certain about this. I'm certain about this. I just didn't want him to walk away like that.

I guess he knows what I really need—which is to put him out of my mind.

I was already talking about forever with Selena before he showed up. What's stopping me?

Nothing is stopping me. I get out of the car and head inside. She's in the kitchen making dinner for both of us.

I see her already acting as my wife. We're living together. Why shouldn't we make it official?

She looks up when I walk in. "Is he okay?"

"He's fine. He likes you a lot. He just wishes we lived closer."

"Maybe that could change sometime."

"You wouldn't want to leave your family. It just means we have to visit more often."

She turns back to the stove to take a pot of boiling water off the burner. She moves her head out of the way and squints when she drains pasta into the colander.

She notices me standing there leaning against the kitchen counter. "Are you okay? Is something on your mind?"

"I was just thinking about our conversation—the conversation we were having about commitment. I want to keep talking about it, now that he's gone."

"Okay. What do you want to talk about it?"

I wait for her to put the pot down. Then I walk over to her and stand extra close so she has no choice but to look up at me. "I want to marry you. That's what I mean by commitment. I don't want to face whatever comes without you by my side. I want to seal the deal and make it work no matter what."

She stares up at me in shock. "You.....you want to get married."

"Yes—but only to you. I wouldn't want to get married just for its own sake. I only want to get married because I'm with you."

She tries to look away. I can't stand that.

I grab her by the chin and steer her face around so she looks at me. "Marry me. Say you want to marry me so we can face all of life's challenges together. Say you don't want to live without me."

Her voice strains in a high-pitched crack of painful emotion. "You know I don't want to live without you. You're everything to me."

"I don't want to live without you, either, baby." I lean in and kiss her. "I *can't* live without you. I already went through that once when you left the cruise ship. Don't make me go through that again. I can't take it."

"I don't want to! I want......" She shuts her eyes tight. "All right. Yes. I'll marry you."

I pull her into my arms and bury my face in her hair. This is all I want—this right here. I can lose all the rest. Aaron is right about that.

She clings to me—exactly the way I cling to her—the way we hold onto each other when we go through all of life's storms.

We can make it. I know we can. We made it through everything that happened before. We can make it through this and everything else.

End of Book 1.

Keep Reading

Paradise Cruises Series: Book 2: Double Cross

Holly Silverman and her husband Carlos came on board the Paradise Cruise ship *Electric Emerald* in the hopes of finally overcoming years of infertility so they can start the family they've always wanted. This cruise could be the secret ingredient that brings them all the happiness they've ever wanted.

Nate Whitman and his wife Alexis came onboard the ship to rekindle their romance and spend some much-needed quality time together after he's been spending so much time away from home traveling around the country for his work.

There's just one problem. Both marriages blow up in the worst possible way when Holly sees Carlos and Alexis hooking up in a back-alley storeroom on board the ship. Did she make a mistake about who she saw or could this be the trigger that tears both couples apart?

The backlash sends all four down a road to destruction none of them could ever have predicted......and the aftermath will leave nothing untouched when all four get called to face what the future holds in store for them.

You can find it at your favorite book retailer.

Sign Up Once--Get all A.E. Moran's free books including brand new releases

The Paradise Cruise ship *Electric Emerald* is buzzing with the news that Stella Lowell is getting married in two days on board the ship. Stella's family, her fiancé Beau, and Beau's family are all on board and over-the-top excited for the big day.

Too bad Stella isn't over-the-top excited for the big day—or for her fiancé and soon to be husband.

The whole catastrophe blows up when Stella's brother Silas interferes with her talking to a man at the bar. It turns out Silas knows Walker Shockley from their time at school together—and Silas has nothing good to say about Walker.

The disastrous results will be far worse than just a wedding nightmare beyond anyone's worst fears. Nothing is what it seems—and no one is what they seem, either. Life has a way of interfering in the best laid plans. Will the result be the life of Stella's dreams or the worst thing that could ever happen to her?

Read it here for free.

Sign up at www.authoraemoran.com to read it for free.

About AE Moran

A .E Moran is the contemporary romance pen name for Theo Mann.

I write 70 books per year—and yes, before you ask, all these books are my original creative work. Nothing written under my name is AI-generated or ghostwritten because I write better than AI and any ghostwriter out there.

People don't read fiction for entertainment or to escape from reality. People read fiction to see their humanity reflected in another person's character and story.

This is my promise to you. When you read my books, you'll see your own humanity reflected in the characters and stories. I take this commitment to my readers very seriously. My books are an intimate form of communication between us. I would never disrespect my readers by turning that over to a machine or another writer. This is my bond between me and you as my reader.

I write 20,000 words per day as my daily work output. If anyone with a public platform would like to challenge me to prove this in a controlled environment, feel free to contact me on this website's contact page. How do I do write so much? Find out more on my blog, *Crimes Against Fiction* at www.theomann.com.

I worked as a professional ghostwriter for fifteen years. Now I'm going for the Guinness World Record by writing 700 books over the next ten years and 1400 books over the next twenty years, all originally written by me.

See my website for the full book list. I'm also the author of *Proof for the Existence of God* and the *Crimes Against Fiction* blog.

You can find out more at www.theomann.com or at www.author aemoran.com.

Also by AE Moran (so far)